Reading Between the Lines

an anthology

by

Bare Writers

First published by Bare Writers 2018

ISBN: 9781727128925

Contents

Vivien Foulkes-James

Vivien started to write poetry as a child growing up in Manchester.

After a varied career in libraries, hospitals and local government. She moved North with her husband and cats to live by the coast. Now, no longer shackled to her employment as a registrar, she is free to spend her time gardening, reading, writing and exploring the countryside.

As a founder member of Bare Writers she enjoys the companionship and support of the group. Vivien is a published poet.

Between The Lines

He walked a lonely path, unable to connect,
he lacked the social glue to hold it all together.
A drifter at school, always the odd boy.

Some thing he had learnt;
to avoid the bullies,
to stay outside the crowd,
one person at a time and
he could just about cope.
He knew that he was different,
he was, "somewhere on the spectrum"
he'd heard the doctor say.
But he could get confused,
there were misinterpretations.
Words emerging out of nowhere,
the blurring of lines and the empty spaces between,
then morphing into something else entirely.
Watching for facial expressions,
a change in the tone of voice,
he tried to read the signs.
And words tumbling out of people's mouths,
and words unspoken, to fill the pauses, the silences
inferred, implicit, but not understood.

"Don't take things at their face value"
a teacher had said,
"learn to read between the lines".

F for Frivolity

Timewasters Welcome
If you always do what you've always done, you'll always get what you've always got. Late 50s M, friendly, cultivated maverick, still got it. Seeks F for frivolity.

I'm early. I hate being anywhere too early. It's a complete waste of time. I'll sit here by the window and try and blend into the background. It's ridiculous that I feel so nervous, I'm like a teenager. I'll try and pretend I'm just like any middle aged woman taking time in her busy day for a cappuccino and a sit down. I've always liked the ambience in Dukes, that's why I suggested it. The people are generally nice.

I'm having doubts now about the outfit. I was trying to get a free thinking slightly hippy look. I may have overdone it. I've gone for a loose ethnic top, not sure about the elephants parading around the bottom, teamed with my terracotta chinos. Too late to do anything about it now, I'll just have to pretend that this is my laid back look.

It's quite busy in here for a Thursday afternoon. Everyone just having a nice normal time, not like me, meeting a potential psychopath. But at least this is neutral ground in a public place. There's supposed to be safety in that.

"If you always do what you've always done, you'll always get what you've always got." I keep thinking about that sentence. It's so obvious really but yet it's thought provoking. Perhaps that's what he had in mind, to make someone think. About their lives and about their future. Well I've done that and I've decided that my life needs a new direction. Could he be part of it? The stakes are almost too high to consider, the thought of happiness too impossible.

To say who you are, your likes and dislikes and who you would hope to be with and their all important qualities, in under 40 words, in code, makes the likelihood of this being a success very remote indeed.

A "friendly, cultivated maverick"! I must admit that I was drawn by that. I even googled maverick, just to be sure. You can't be too careful can you, these days. Some people are so weird. "Individualist, non-conformist, free spirit, unorthodox person", is what it came up with. Well, I quite like the sound of that, I consider myself a free spirit. Unorthodox person, could cover a number of possibilities though. At least he says he's cultivated, so that's something I suppose.

Apparently, he's "still got it". I wonder what the 'it' in question is and more to the point how soon is he going to want to use it!

It's five past now, punctuality can't be one of his strong points. I'm beginning to think this was all a dreadful mistake. I must be out of my mind, arranging a date with a complete stranger.

Do I seek "frivolity"? I'm not sure, most people think I'm quite serious. I'm certainly in need of some frivolity, it's been such a long time since any came my way.

I think it's all a wind-up, he did say time wasters welcome. That must be the joke, he isn't going to show up.

I'll wait another five minutes and then that's it. I'm furious really, all the time and effort I've put in, OMG I think this must be him, he's smiling, he's walking over here, striding purposefully. Oh no …

Timewasters Welcome

Timewasters Welcome
If you always do what you've always done, you'll always get what you've always got. Late 50s M, friendly, cultivated maverick, still got it. Seeks F for frivolity.

Is it all a waste of time? This search for someone new at my time of life?

This is woman number three on my shortlist. I'm not expecting too much this time. Maybe that's been my problem, expectations too high. The first woman, Vicky, sounded ideal, right from her very first email. I was convinced we were a perfect match. The reality proved somewhat different. She was loud and bossy. A combination I could do without. Years of living with Stella have made me very wary of women like Vicky.

My second assignment was a disaster too, but in a different way. Such a pretty name, it conjured up the idea of someone young, different, exciting even. Tamsin was a perfectly nice woman but there was no physical attraction, no spark. Short in stature and with thick muscular arms and no doubt legs to match, but thankfully they weren't on display. I towered over her as we made our obligatory goodbye hug, her head nestling briefly on my all too evident paunch. I'm ashamed to admit to being so shallow, but I actually felt repelled by her.

So, could it be third time lucky or should I

give in, admit defeat. Go back home to Connemara to spend the rest of my days with a lovely Irish woman met in the more natural, haphazard, old fashioned way.

I spent hours composing that advert. Trying to convey the essence of my personality. OK I admit it, I was trying to be clever, to tease out my dream date. I used a bit of artistic licence, of course. I thought late fifties had a better ring to it. Friendly, well sometimes, depending on mood and the company I'm in.

Cultivated maverick, I thought was a stroke of genius. It certainly got results. Who would have thought there were so many free spirits out there and most of them lonely and wanting the company of a man in his late fifties.

One hundred and forty three replies after one week. That took some sorting out. From the mildly eccentric to the plain bonkers. Frivolity may have been a mistake. There were a crop of bubbly ladies with GSOH. I discounted them straight away.

I'm running late now, was the bus a good idea? You can never rely on them to get you anywhere on time. At least she won't be waiting outside, Dukes Café Bar was a good choice, hers of course. I don't think I would have thought of a mid-afternoon date, but maybe there's less pressure.

I need to get fit, I'll just get my breath back before I go in. Rushing up from the station has made me all sweaty, not the look I was after at all.

"Hi there, I'm Cormac you must be Annie ..."

Letters From Jersey

Hotel Jardin
St Helier
17/18 April 2018

Dear Sylvia

Thought I'd surprise you with a letter. Too much to put into a text. At last, you'll be thinking, for once in her life she's taken my advice! As you'll have noticed, I'm away on holiday. Alone! I'm spending some time here in St Helier to try and recover and give myself time to think. It's absolutely beautiful, I don't know why I haven't been to Jersey before.

You have spent so long listening to my problems, you must be sick to death of it. I don't know how you've put up with me, I must apologise. I know you've always been sceptical that Martin would ever leave his wife, but for all these years, it's what I've been living for. We'd got away with it for so long that we must have become careless and quite blasé to the risks we were running. I suppose it had to end sometime, it was just a matter of when. To end up in that showdown was awful, I don't think I'll ever feel safe in my own home again.

I had to take time off work with the torn tendons and it was a little awkward explaining to my boss just exactly how the injuries had come about.

But she surprised me by saying I mustn't rush back to work, they can manage perfectly well without me. Quite sweet really I suppose. I had several weeks of annual leave due to me so I added them on to the sick leave and thought I could recuperate here in Jersey. A complete change of scene, some space to rethink my future. I managed to get the front door and windows repaired before I left. I think I've swung it with the insurance company, but they were suspicious. They asked me all sorts of tricky questions but luckily it was all done by phone so they couldn't see my facial expressions. I'm sure they'd have given me away.

The hotel is fab, 5 star with an outdoor pool, complete with jacuzzi and waterslide. I've been in it twice and already I'm beginning to feel the benefit. I've noticed that most of the staff in the hotels and cafes here are male, mainly French and so polite and courteous. I do feel better here, it's just that I'm so not looking forward to going back home. They're putting on a special 1950s evening in the hotel tonight. I think I might go, it sounds like fun. I've got my navy dress with me that could pass off as vaguely fifties and I could always go and get my hair done.

Sylvia, you won't believe what a marvellous time I had last night. I sat alone at my table for one. There was a charming young waiter, Henri, who was most attentive. I took his recommendation on the wine, a Rioja, lovely, he was so informative. He said he could tell I appreciated the finer things in life. That French accent is such a turn on. The jazz band played and I couldn't believe how my emotions could ricochet from feeling so low when I arrived to now feeling so elated. Henri complimented me on my dress, he said I looked like Audrey Hepburn. I had my hair done a little differently, I think I'll keep it like this.

A man who said his name was Roger came over and asked me to dance, who'd have guessed that I still had it in me? I must say all this male attention is quite therapeutic, I've been wasted on Martin. Anyway, I was a little apprehensive, not having danced for such a long time but I soon got into it. Well, the band was playing and the wine helped. Roger asked me to join him and his friends at their table but I declined, politely. I wanted to get back to my table for one and back to Henri.

As I came up to bed last night, Bewitched, Bothered and Bewildered was still going round in my head. I slept like I haven't done in ages, a deep and happy sleep.

Henri and I have exchanged mobile numbers and although I know nothing can come of it, I feel so excited, like a girl again. I'm just about to go down for breakfast now and it's another glorious day, just perfect for exploring more of the island. Can't wait to see Henri later, when he's off duty.

Hope everything's fine with you.

I'll ring you when I get back and tell you all, in detail.

Best love

Tessa

PS. Sylvia, you won't believe it! I've just had a text from Martin, says his wife has agreed to take him back but he's 'missing me *sooo* much', poor love!

Top Flat
52 Queens Road
St Helier

4 May 2018

Dear Sylvia

I know, I know, I should have written before, you must have been wondering what's been happening to me. It's all been a bit of a whirlwind really.

Henri persuaded me to stay on here in St Helier. Well, I didn't take much persuading it's such a lovely place and with Henri for company, how could I say no.

I've moved into Henri's flat for now as the hotel was proving a bit expensive. It's a little cramped as it's only designed for one person. Henri goes back home to Rouen every couple of weeks. He says his mother misses him so much and he is such a dutiful son he doesn't like to disappoint her. I'm hoping to go with him soon as I'd love to meet her.

He has shown me all his favourite parts of the island. I'm beginning to feel a bit more like a local now.

Sylvia, you must come over and visit me here, I know you'll love it. I'm sure you'll be charmed by Henri, he is such a gentleman and his accent is something else!

You'll never believe what I'm doing now to earn my keep. Asparagus picking! Yes I know, it's not my usual line of work but I was really taken with the ad for the job. I am working at Dingle Dell Farm, sounds delightful doesn't it, so rural. It's quite hard work, the hours are long and it's not having a good effect on my nail extensions but I'm looking on it as a temporary measure. They did say that applicants had to be fit but I'm not sure how much longer my knees will be able to take it.

I have put in an application for a Spa Receptionist at one of the hotels here. It sounds great as I could benefit from all the treatments they offer. Also this one comes with accommodation which would solve my housing problem too. I'm sure I'll get something more suitable soon. I've updated my CV and I think my varied career history should stand me in good stead.

I must tell you about Martin. It's ironic really that I was at his beck and call for years while he spent the rest of his time cosied up with his wife and family. All I wanted was for him to leave them so that we could be a couple legitimately without all the subterfuge. Now he is desperate for me to go back home and is threatening to come over here to see me. How I could have put up with this for so long I can't imagine now.

I must close now as Henri is due home from his shift at the hotel and I have to try to get the dirt from under my nails and make myself beautiful for his return. Although sometimes he's so whacked from his hotel duties he doesn't seem to notice me, he's asleep as soon as his head hits the pillow, ah bless him.

Best love

Tessa

Top Flat
52 Queens Road
St Helier

18 May 2018

Dear Sylvia

So good to get your text. I'm glad my letters are such a source of amusement for you, perhaps I should start writing a blog. Letters from Jersey, it has a certain ring to it, don't you think? Who knows, it could become a source of income for me. I could certainly do with it just now.

I've given up the asparagus picking. Seems like agriculture was not a wise career move for me. Well actually, I was asked to leave. Kenny, the owner of Dingle Dell Farm, said he didn't think I was cut out for the job. He was concerned for my well being, which is sweet of him I know, but I do need to get something else pretty smartish. I'm pinning all my hopes on an interview I've got next Thursday for Spa Receptionist at the Pandora Hotel. It could be the answer to all my problems, an interesting job meeting new people as well as all the perks of the treatments on offer plus accommodation. Sounds perfect!

Henri thinks I need to get my own place now. He loves having me here but his flat is so pokey, there's nowhere to put my clothes, most I'm having to keep in my case apart from one or two items I've managed to squeeze into his wardrobe. The evenings when he's at work are a bit lonely. It's lucky I've got my laptop.

Do you remember Judith Wright from school? She friended me on Facebook and now she's talking of coming over here next weekend to see me. I struggle to think of anything we'll have in common, I remember her as a timid mousey girl. I can hardly believe the profile of her now, some high powered job on the South coast. Strangely, she seems to have done very well for herself. Who would have predicted that?

Did I tell you, I cycle everywhere here? No need for a car the island is so small. Also it's part of my keep fit regime. I imagine that all the staff at the Spa will be lithe young things, I don't want to be made to feel old and frumpy. I've been to some yoga classes on the beach. It's a wonderful way to keep supple and I'm aiming to drop two dress sizes.

Henri has promised that when he has a weekend off, we'll take the ferry to St Malo. I'd love to visit his home and meet his mother, he talks so fondly of her. But he wants to show me the sights and take me to this lovely little restaurant he knows. He says there may not be time to do everything this trip. I'm not sure when this will happen, weekends are the busiest time for him at the hotel. They run him ragged at that place, poor love.

Just had another message from Judith, she's booked her ticket and wants me to meet her at the airport. I really could do without this at the moment. I need to concentrate on getting a job and somewhere to live, not wasting time with someone I never got on with forty years ago. Also, I'm not sure if she'll approve of Henri. He is quite a bit younger than me, did I mention that?

Wish me luck with my interview, I'll need it, there's a lot depending on it.

Best love

Tessa

PS Just told Henri about Judith coming over, he thinks I should catch up with old friends, he says it will be good for me. He said he'd like to meet her. I can't see that going well …

Mrs Beasley's Guesthouse
Main Street
St Helier

4 June 2018

Dear Sylvia

What a week! Talk about an emotional rollercoaster. Where to begin? I went to meet Judith and as you know, I was not looking forward to seeing her at all. Things were a little awkward to begin with. I was taken aback by her, she was so confident and stylish. Not anything like the girl I knew in Miss Sumner's class. We came back here, I'd booked us both into Mrs Bs Guesthouse. Things were a bit fraught at Henri's flat. The lack of space was beginning to be an issue between us.

We went out for lunch by the waterfront. We had a lot of catching up to do. She told me all about her job, she's Director of Wellbeing, what a title, sounds so important doesn't it. She's freelance and has some very high powered and celebrity clients. But she's very clever and such a good listener. I opened up to her like I haven't done with anyone before. She's got "listening skills". I told her all about Martin and how I'd put my life on hold just waiting for him to leave his wife. Then about Henri and how he was such a breath of fresh air when I first came to Jersey, although lately we had been having some problems. I surprised myself by the things I was saying. She was so understanding.

Henri had manged to swap shifts so that he was free for the evening. I could see immediately that he was impressed by Judith and of course, he was absolutely charming, as I knew he would be. We had a lovely meal and afterwards went for a walk along the bay. Judith and Henri were deep in conversation and I kept getting on ahead and then having to wait for them to catch up. They seemed to hit it off so I needn't have worried on that score. Henri even took one of Judith's business cards, he said he might need her services at some point.

Anyway the upshot is, I saw Judith off at the airport on Monday evening. I feel like my life has been transformed in just one weekend. Honestly Sylvia, you won't believe how Judith has made me rethink and re-evaluate my life. There's so much to take in, mindfulness, goal-setting and personal growth. She thinks I should start with behaviour modification. She says I was used by Martin and she thinks maybe Henri isn't all he pretends to be. She thinks I shouldn't pin all my hopes for happiness on men. That way lies disaster, Judith says. I should aim high. I shouldn't be wasting my time with jobs such as receptionist and asparagus picking. That is a waste of my talents, according to Judith.

I feel so liberated and re-energised. I'm

packing up and coming back home at the end of the week. I'm going to sort things out, put my house on the market and make a fresh start on the South coast. Judith says I can move into her place while I look for somewhere. She said she'll help me with my job search. I'm so excited by the prospect of my new life. Got a few things to tie up here before I leave. Mainly, telling Henri. It's not going to be easy, he'll be heartbroken I know but it's the right thing to do. The sooner I can start modifying my behaviour the better and holiday romances rarely succeed, do they.

I'll text you when I'm back home Sylvia. *Sooo* looking forward to seeing you.

Big hugs

Tessa

PS Just had a text from Judith. She's fixed me up with a job interview with one of her clients, they're looking for a Director of First Impressions! Sounds brilliant - can't wait.

#MeToo

Sir,

It is with a heavy heart that I write this letter to you, but I see no other course of action open to me.

When first I came here twelve months ago, I was so grateful to you. Finally, I thought I had found a place where I could be comfortable and earn my keep doing the job that I was trained for. Adele is a sweet little thing and learns well but long hours spent with only a child for company left me craving for conversation of a more adult nature. Knowing your dislike of gossip I adhered to your instructions not to engage with the other staff. I have felt lonely at times, but always I could return here to this room. I have my books and occasional letters to write. I must admit that I was flattered you sought me out and I looked forward to the time we spent together. I thought it was a meeting of minds, but I see now, you wanted so much more.

It pains me to say this but, I have to call a halt to our friendship. You are more than twice my age, you are my employer. You hold all the cards, this is not a union of equals.

Glancing round this room now, which has been my sanctuary, I can hardly comprehend that this will be my last night here. The candles and the last embers in the grate show the room in such a pretty light making my leaving all the more painful.

By first light I will be gone.

Now all is silent apart from the easterly wind whistling through the casements and the scratching of my pen on this notepaper as I write to seal my fate. But very soon there will be the disturbances from the upper floor and try as I have done to ignore it, sleep is impossible until the commotion subsides.

This house holds its secrets. Questions hang unanswered in the corridors, whispers echo from room to room and the treads of the backstairs keep their terrible truths.

Tomorrow I shall leave here and throw myself on the mercy of my aunt until such time as I can secure another position as governess. That will be my future.

Sir, I could never marry. I had only one true love and she was cruelly taken from me.

Forgive me and try to understand.

Respectfully,

Jane

Peter Clarke

After a long career in the telecommunications industry, Peter felt the need for a change. He and his wife swapped the gentle landscapes of Suffolk for the more rugged terrain (and weather) of the North of England where he is starting to build a second career as a writer and artist. Peter's inspiration comes from finding the remarkable in the mundane and seeking the rare in the commonplace.

The Commission

The Robinsons' house was difficult to find. From the road a copse of oak trees, still bearing the autumn colours, hid any form of habitation. All that could be seen was a small dirt track that extended from the roadside, skirting behind the trees and extending over a small hill. Evidently, the family that lived here did not welcome uninvited guests. Fortunately, Aaron had both an invitation and a sketch map showing their location.

Aaron's car struggled with the dirt track and inwardly he cursed the Robinsons for their lack of consideration in not having the path suitably surfaced. Then again, he rather imagined both the Robinsons and their more usual guests would drive upmarket 4x4s rather than his ten year old ratty estate car with worn tyres. The car shook and shimmied along and over the track, bringing Aaron to a rather extensive paved area that marked the front of the property.

The house was large. A detached three storey Victorian dwelling that, at one time, might have served as a guest house. To the side of the property and looking a little out of place in such a genteel setting was a Range Rover SUV in a garish Savannah Orange colour.

Aaron parked at its side, stepped out of his car and picked up a duffle bag from the passenger side which he hoisted onto his shoulder. On walking to the house, the thought briefly crossed his mind that he should seek a tradesman's entrance. He walked hesitantly to the front of the house and stood before the door. Aaron straightened his well-worn jacket, turning the sleeve to hide a paint stain on the cuff and pushed his mop of hair in place. After a final check of the state of his shoes, he pushed the doorbell. This was the nose of a large polished brass lion's head ornament which served to guard the entrance of the dwelling. Aaron absently noted that the melancholic expression of the lion seemed to echo something of his own emotions at the prospect of being here.

In the time it took to shuffle, fidget, decide on a suitably business like, yet nonchalant pose, the door was opened by a man in his fifties, dressed in black jeans and a faded sweatshirt.

"Yes?" asked the man as he looked at Aaron with some suspicion.

"Aaron Chandler, artist. You invited me to discuss a painting."

The man bared his teeth in a grimace which suggested he was not used to smiling, and extended his hand for Aaron to shake.

"Yes, come in. We are expecting you."

Aaron shook the proffered hand and entered a rather gloomy hallway. A pair of discarded Wellington boots lay to the side of the door and the floor was uncarpeted, exposing well-worn floor boards. Instinctively he knew there would be an Aga cooker alight in the kitchen, and Aaron was rather surprised not to find a couple of dogs bounding to greet him.

"Go through to the living room, first on the right," said the man as he closed the front door and followed Aaron down the hallway. "You will find my wife in there."

Aaron found himself in a spacious room with a large window that allowed plenty of light and looked out onto a magnificent view of the Lake District, with Coniston Water just visible in the distance. The room was rather spartan in its furnishings. A chest of drawers occupied one corner and there was a coal fireplace on the inside wall in which a fire burned merrily. Numerous pictures of the rather 'chocolate box' variety decorated most of the wall, depicting landscapes or scenes from major European cities. In front of the window lay a large table and seated at this, gazing out of the window was Mrs Robinson. Aaron guessed her age as mid to late thirties. She had straight black hair with just a hint of grey, and the hair extended to her shoulders. She wore a simple yet elegant dress that complemented her classical features. As she rose to greet Aaron, she moved with the ease that suggested frequent yoga workouts or ballet lessons as a child.

"Mr Chandler," said the man. "This is my

wife Lucy. I wish you to paint her portrait."

"Very pleased to meet you," said Aaron, quite truthfully, as Lucy smiled at him. "I'd be delighted to try to paint you."

"My wife will supply all information regarding times and dates for sittings," said Mr Robinson in a rather off-hand manner. "So I will leave the two of you to chat. When you have finished, come and find be in the library so we can discuss finances."

With that, Mr Robinson glanced at his wife, gave Aaron a dismissive nod and left the room, leaving both artist and sitter together.

#

Lucy gave a warm smile, lounged back into her chair and motioned to an empty seat. Aaron relaxed into the chair by her side.

"So, Mrs Robinson, what do you have in mind?"

"Call me Lucy." She sighed and a haunted look flashed momentarily across her face.

"I'm rather surprised that my husband arranged for you to come, it's a little out of his character." She paused, as if choosing her words carefully. "Yes I would like a portrait."

"Do you have a preference for the medium?" asked Aaron. Lucy looked puzzled.

"An oil painting, acrylic, watercolour,"

"Oil would be good."

"Very fitting, a classic medium for a portrait," said Aaron as he found himself starting to warm to the task in hand.

"And what of style?"

Lucy smiled, but said nothing.

"A formal pose with you in a stately dress, or perhaps a rather more contemporary approach, with more adventurous colours and perhaps a less formal outfit?"

Lucy hesitated again and gave him a more intense stare, while she briefly nibbled her bottom lip. "Aaron, can I leave the details with you? I'll agree to whatever you think is best. But I would like to have something by which the world will remember me. My whole life seems to have been defined by my appearance. Did you know I was once a beauty queen?"

Aaron shook his head.

"Despite a strong Catholic upbringing, my mother encouraged me, perhaps pushed me into modelling, but I never found the big break. Then, I met and married an older man. I guess he fell for my looks, but it's not much of a career being a trophy wife. With the passage of years, I find my looks are starting to fade and I fear I'm losing all of me."

Aaron squirmed in his chair, desperately trying to think of something to say, but in the end said nothing.

"So, I want to make a statement of what I was

and all I could have been. I want to leave something behind that shows me at my best. I don't know enough of art to discuss the details. Can you paint me a portrait that will give me, a legacy?" Wiping away a small tear from the corner of her eye, Lucy looked intently at Aaron for a couple of seconds.

"Yes," said Aaron quietly, "I think I can give you that."

Lucy gave a contented sigh and relaxed even further into her chair, her eyes taking in the view from the window. "I would like to have the work done in this room. It's where I spend most of my time and where I feel most relaxed. Of all the house, this is my space. Besides, the window admits a good light. I seem to go outside so infrequently now."

"Of course, here will be ideal. Can I ask how you typically spend your time, your interests? It might make for a better portrait if you were doing something or surrounded by something that has significance to you."

Lucy gave a fleeting sad shrug. "I spend my time dreaming about travel. Have you seen much of the world? I haven't. I explore the major cities in my mind. I collect jigsaw puzzles showing views of the capitals of Europe and, as I'm putting the pieces together, I feel like I'm walking the streets and taking in the culture. The finished puzzles, are on display."

Aaron realised the pictures on the walls which he disparaged earlier were in fact framed jigsaw puzzles. She pointed to the jigsaw on the table in front of her.

"This is Venice. I've never been there but would love to board a gondola and go to St. Mark's Square to explore." Lucy stared out of the window, apparently lost in the loneliness of her own thoughts. Breaking the silence, Aaron simply said,

"I can paint you at work at this table." In his mind, Aaron pictured Lucy sitting at a right angle to the window, so that the light would cast a soft shadow across the far side of her face to accentuate her delicate nose and the sensuous curve of her neck and cleavage. The partially completed jigsaw, laid out in front of her would symbolise Lucy's broken view of the world and she could hold a piece of the puzzle in her hand to symbolise her innocence and youth. This would contrast with the maturity of the side of her face facing the light. The whole would represent a woman who also was a child. Such a scene might tax Aaron's skills as a painter, but he could, he would, make it work. The end result would be a stunning tribute to this extraordinary and rather ethereal woman.

"Can we start today?" asked Aaron. "Perhaps I could make a quick charcoal sketch, just to try out an idea. If this pleases you, we could arrange a date to begin in earnest with oils."

Lucy shook herself from her reverie, smiled, and gave a delicate nod.

"If you could sit here, facing the table."

Lucy located to where Aaron had indicated and he moved his chair so that he had a three-quarters view of his model, including the top of the table and partially completed jigsaw.

"Just get comfortable, relax as if you were going to continue with the puzzle. Take a piece in your hand and look to see where it might fit and that's it. Excellent. If you can hold that position for about twenty minutes, then we will take a break." Aaron took a sketchbook from his duffle bag, resting it on his knee. Taking a large block of charcoal, he proceeded to cover the page with a thin, uniform layer of pigment. Thence, with a chamois leather, he wiped away the charcoal to represent the highlights of the illuminated side of her face. With a second, thinner stick of charcoal he added darks where her face was in deeper shadow.

"If you don't mind my asking Lucy, why don't you travel?" His model initially looked up, but remembering she was supposed to be posing, she returned her eyes to the jigsaw.

"I can't travel. My husband doesn't like me to leave him and he is too busy with his business interests to take a vacation. Besides, he has visited his share of foreign cities to attend meetings. If, when he retires, I'm sure we will tour Europe. Until then I have put my ambitions on hold."

With the initial layer of charcoal acting as the mid-tone, Aaron delineated her eyes, observing she used just a hint of eye shadow. He sketched the delicacy of her nose and the fullness of her lips. Lucy was able to keep still, despite the conversation and was looking intently at the jigsaw piece she held in her hand.

"And Mr Robinson, what does he do?"

Lucy sat silent for a moment, as if weighing up her answer. "My husband is out most days. He made a fortune in the city and now sits on a couple of boards. In the evening, he is normally to be found in the library which he uses as a study. You will see him there shortly."

Aaron felt he had captured something of her expression and so concentrated on rendering the form of her hand, always a tricky part of the anatomy, as it hovered over the desk and the unfinished puzzle. "Yet with a house this size, surely you must have many guests, dinner parties, dances even."

"When we were first married, we did a lot of entertaining. That was a time of new dresses and extravagant parties. In the summer months we'd have a marquee in the garden and have caterers in to prepare buffets or the occasional barbecue. That was the time when we'd just moved here and we were getting established in the North of England. But it didn't last. I guess he, we, got older and more set in our ways. Now we are much less adventurous in our socialising."

Aaron gently sucked air between his teeth as he took a final look at the sketch. After a moment, he turned the sketch pad to the model so she could see the result. "This is just a quick trial, a cross between a working drawing and a first stab at capturing your likeness. If we were to develop this idea into a full blown oil, is that the sort of thing that you had in mind?"

Lucy examined the sketch intently from across the table for a few seconds. She rose and came to Aaron to get a closer look and a warm smile spread across her face. "Why Aaron, yes that is what I have in mind. If I'd known you were going to start work now, I would have worn a more elegant dress and combed my hair." As she continued to look at the sketch, it was Aaron's turn to smile. For the first time he knew that the commission was going to be successful.

"Let's leave it here today," said Aaron. "The next time we meet, I'll bring easel and oils so we can make a start on the real work."

"This weekend?" asked Lucy.

"Saturday afternoon?" countered Aaron.

"It's a date!" Lucy laughed at her own words.

#

Aaron had no trouble finding the library as the door to the room had a plaque on it bearing the legend

'Library', printed in Blackletter Gothic script. He knocked gently and entered.

Mr Robinson was seated in a leather chair behind a large desk that faced the library door. He was nursing a glass of whisky in one hand, whilst reading a newspaper that he had spread out over the desk top. This seemed to be of great interest to him, as Mr Robinson briefly held up a finger, bidding Aaron to wait whilst he continued to read. This gave Aaron a chance to examine the room in detail. Bookshelves were erected on two of the walls of the room and pride of place was given to an immaculate print edition of the Encyclopaedia Britannica. The majority of other books were collections of classic literature, Dickens, Hawthorne, Tolkien and Shakespeare. There was also a shelf devoted to Fleming. All were in pristine condition. One shelf housed reference books, a dictionary, thesaurus and an atlas, which showed some signs of wear. On a third wall hung a large TV set, tuned into a 24 hour news channel, the volume muted. The final wall had a window, shaded by trees, that overlooked the driveway to the house.

Mr Robinson finished the newspaper article and inspected Aaron.

"How did you like my wife, Mr Chandler."

"She will make a great model," responded Aaron, "and she seemed genuinely excited at the prospect of having her portrait commissioned. With your permission, we intend to start the work in earnest over the coming weekend and I've already made a quick sketch to explore ideas for a pose. Would you like to see?" Aaron held out his sketch pad to Mr Robinson, but the latter made no move to take the book. Rather he took a sip of the whisky and continued to stare at Aaron.

"Do you know why I selected you to paint this portrait?"

"No," said Aaron slowly, as he placed his sketchbook, open, on the edge of the desk. "I'd assumed you had seen some of my work, perhaps at a recent exhibition, and come to like my style."

"I don't attend art exhibitions, Mr Chandler. I find the whole subject rather frivolous. Art is a commodity to be bought and sold, an investment and little more." He paused, rolling the glass of whisky in his hand. "No Mr Chandler, I chose you because of your rather perilous financial state. I know your landlord, he and I did some business once and I know he could be induced to raise your rent. These days Mr Chandler, there is so little protection for anyone who is not financially secure. I'm told you have talent, but you share the poverty that so often accompanies the talented artist."

Mr Robinson took another small sip of his drink, whilst Aaron squirmed in the awkward silence.

"My wife," continued Mr Robinson, "does

not appreciate the benefit of her position. She was beautiful once, and I'm told she is attractive still. But fading looks do not give her the right to." He paused. "I am the man who pays the piper, Mr Chandler, and I will call the tune. You are to take my wife's looks away."

The hairs rose on Aaron's neck and he felt a chill run through him.

"I don't think I follow."

"In the portrait, I want you to show every wrinkle, embellish every imperfection, emphasise every asymmetry of my wife's face. Use the full range of your considerable talent Mr Chandler to create a likeness of my wife, but one that seeps poison. And for your recompense,"

Mr Robinson emptied his glass, placing the tumbler gently on the top of the desk.

"For your recompense, I will pay a sum of ten thousand pounds for a portrait that meets my specific requirements. In addition, I am in a position to recommend your services to a number of my business clients and I'm sure they will offer you further work. However if you cross me Mr Chandler, if you produce a portrait that gives my wife joy, you will find me very creative in ensuring your poverty."

Aaron's immediate impulse was to storm out of the house, possibly after punching his host. Using art in such a petty and vindictive way repulsed him and he wanted no part in the matter. However Mr Robinson was correct in the assessment of his financial position. Aaron lacked the security that comes from a steady income and mentally he listed the outstanding bills that could be settled with a ten thousand pounds payment. He also felt sure that Mr Robinson could and would make life difficult for him if he were to refuse this commission. Hence Aaron remained speechless for some seconds as he tried to settle on a response. In the end he managed to blurt out only "I will consider your proposal."

#

In the early hours after a restless night, Aaron was dressed in paint-splattered jeans and T shirt. The early morning was not a time that he enjoyed, but he had awoken from a half remembered dream involving his being chased by something unpleasant. Now, fully awake before six, he had decided to get dressed and start the day. Oblivious to the pervading smell of turpentine, he nursed a cup of strong black coffee that stuck to his hand where his fingers had picked up traces of oil. Sitting on a well-worn settee in his studio, he contemplated his options.

The past month had been busy, yet emotionally exhausting. He had visited the Robinsons' house on numerous occasions to meet with Lucy, and had been able to generate a series of working sketches, with her dressed in different gowns, trying different poses, and adopting different expressions. Aaron's feelings towards her were ambivalent, but mainly positive. She was certainly charming and with a mischievous sense of humour. However, whether by disposition or by the consequence of her lifestyle, she seemed to have lost her self-determination and resilience. Initially Aaron had come to despise Mr Robinson as an arrogant bully. However, during the subsequent meetings, Aaron's anger had transformed more into pity as he came to see Mr Robinson more as a declining force. A man without passion who was trying to come to terms with the absence of power in his life, which was manifest as jealousy of the beauty of his younger wife.

Yet what to do? Aaron could just about afford to turn down the commission, but he couldn't risk a rise in rent for his accommodation and studio. Thus he was not able to refuse the option for a 'poisoned portrait'. Also, the artistic difficulty of producing a work which both captured the likeness of the sitter, yet showed only ugliness and distortion, this was a challenge to his virtuosity. As an intellectual puzzle, this was something that Aaron felt he had to solve, a test of his skills and a proof of his ability. Hence, this task had been the objective of two weeks of intense work. He had completed the portrait last night but had turned it towards the wall before retiring to a disturbed night's sleep. With a sigh Aaron rose, walked to the malign painting and placed it on his easel to see if the image still seemed to work in the cold light of morning. The portrait showed Lucy seated with the jigsaw as he had originally envisaged. Yet rather than show a mixture of innocence and maturity, the work conveyed indifference and defeat. The side of her face illuminated by light from the window captured the imperfections of her features, with a myriad of fine wrinkles casting small but distinct shadows. The eye was clear but lacked the sparkle of humanity, showing a dead gaze. The side of the face hidden by shadow lacked clarity of features but hinted at the flabbiness of tired muscle with the approach of old age. The eye on this side of the face seemed to convey the despair of someone wasting time with childish puzzles to compensate for the absence of loving family and convivial friends. The choice of the background clashed with the colour of Lucy's skin suggesting an artificial, almost plastic texture to her hands and face. Also the depiction of her clothes hinted more at sated passion than childlike innocence. Yet, the whole was easily recognisable as an excellent likeness of Lucy with neither nose, mouth, eyes nor any other component part showing any sign of exaggeration or distortion. It was in the assemblage of all the features of the sitter that the malevolence of the image lay. In all, the artwork was a masterpiece of malice and Aaron was rather disturbed to find he could take a pride in his ability to produce such a work.

Aaron set up a second easel to the side of the first and placed on this a second, earlier portrait of Lucy, executed on wood rather than canvas. This was the one he had initially wanted to paint. This portrait was an equally good likeness of Lucy and again showed the sitter at the desk in contemplation of a puzzle. But now the model was seen in a positive light. The painting emphasised her humanity and hinted at her desire to travel. Her eyes in this second work shone with the hope that her life would change and her demeanour conveyed a latent energy that would ensure she found success in anything that she tried.

Two portraits done, but what was the next step?

#

Some days later two packages arrived at the Robinsons' household. The first, addressed to Mr Robinson, was a framed copy of the malignant portrait, with an invoice enclosed for the sum agreed for the work. The second parcel was addressed to Mrs Robinson and this was a cardboard box containing a jigsaw puzzle. However, it was unlike any puzzle Lucy had seen before as there were over 500 pieces and each formed part of an oil painting. Yet on the front of the box was a picture of a bible, lying on a table, open at the gospel of John and showing the quote in bold text, “Ye shall know the truth, and the truth shall make you free.”

Leah Jean Lindsay

Leah enjoyed a long and successful career as a hard working hairdresser and salon owner, learning a lot about the human condition at the same time.

After retiring she studied creative writing at Lancaster University and has had many of her stories and poems published in magazines and anthologies. She lives in Bare with her husband, Jack, and loves to walk the coastal paths in all weathers.

Blue Suede Shoes

They've been around, these shoes,
suede isn't serviceable
you told me so
but I would have them – loved the colour.
They've moulded themselves to every bone and bunion
on my feet.
Neat?
Certainly not,
but loved
oh yes.
Lasted longer than you and me
and well travelled
halfway round the world together
and the laces are only just beginning to fray.

Walking Digby

It wasn't as if I'd really wanted the dog.

'You'll be lonely now that Kate's gone,' they all said. 'A dog will get you out, keep you going, give you something to care for.'

Had I been honest, I would have told them that I was actually enjoying not having anything to care for. Kate had been my soul mate. We'd been married for forty years, so of course I cared for her willingly because I loved her, and although I missed her, I rather enjoyed the selfish way of life doing exactly as I pleased.

Anyway, that's how Digby the dachshund came to live with me and although he was a blooming nuisance at times, I suppose I quite liked him. He was a rescue dog, so he needed company as much as I evidently did. Walks were not too strenuous, his little legs didn't stretch very far even though he could at times pick up a bit of speed, and once the back end business had been sorted out he was quite happy to return home with me and go to sleep on the sofa.

Anyway, last Sunday morning we ventured out for a wet, soggy walk. I would have much preferred a lie in and a quiet read of the papers but a dog's needs are non - negotiable so I fastened Digby's gaberdine mac over his fat little belly and he set off in his usual jaunty manner. The fields where we usually took our walks looked a bit wet and muddy and as I said before Digby's little legs were not conducive to long wet grass so that's why I opened the gate and entered the graveyard ignoring the sign that said 'No Dogs.'

The paths were newly laid with tarmac and Digby fairly galloped along, excited to be outside in the fresh air, and so, probably unwisely, I unclipped his lead to give him more freedom. Suddenly he veered off the path to the right onto a smaller path, took another right turn and disappeared into the long wet grass. I groaned. It was beginning to rain even heavier, this was all I needed. 'Digby!' I shouted loudly, maybe too loudly for a quiet church yard. 'Digby come here!'

I looked down at my shoes. They were the blue suede that Kate had told me not to buy, not really suitable for traipsing around in long wet grass. How stupid was I? She always said I was like a child that needed dressing. But I'd no choice I had to find that pesky dog, and I launched my blue suede into the wet grass.

As I wove my way between the grave stones I began to hear an exited yelping. That was Digby, I knew it, what on earth had he found, a dead pigeon? I followed the commotion and found him in the arms of a woman, a very attractive woman I might add, and for some strange reason she had tears streaming down her face. On the floor beside her was a bottle of water that had been knocked over, a vase, and a bunch of red roses. I stood and stared at the tableaux in front of me. 'You obviously know Digby then?'

She looked up at me, even though she was crying she had beautiful eyes. 'Of course I know Digby, he was our dog. But my husband died and because I work abroad a lot it was impossible for me to keep him, but I've missed him so much.'

Digby continued to lick her face and yelp with excitement. I'd never seen him so happy.

She frowned. 'Are you his new owner?'

I nodded.

'And do you love him?

'Well, love's a very strong word but I enjoy his company.'

'But not the morning walks in the rain.'

I gave a guilty laugh. 'Well, no, actually.'

'I'm retiring in two months, I could take him back.'

I was shocked at that. Did I really want to give him back? What about the way he snuggled up to me on the sofa when I watched television. Or what about the way he liked to sneak into my bedroom and sleep on the end of the bed. 'I don't want to confuse the little fella any more than he has been,' I said. 'But we could talk about it.'

She kissed his nose. 'I've missed you so much, Digby.'

It was a bit of a mad idea but then I said, 'If

you really wanted him back you would have to keep in touch with him.'

'How could I do that?

'You could come round to my place for dinner once a week if you're in the country.'

She looked uneasy. 'I'm a strict vegetarian.'

I smiled. 'What a coincidence, so am I.'

Her eyes widened.

'I don't live far away. Do you fancy a coffee? We can dry out and you can spend some time with Digby?'

She smiled. What lovely teeth, and her eyes sparkled, what lovely eyes. I clipped Digby's lead onto his collar and handed her the lead. 'My name's Michael by the way.'

'Oh, I'm Laura,' she said.

I waited until she put the remains of the water and the roses into the vase and we walked out of the churchyard with the dog between us. We sat for ages over our coffee but eventually she said she had to go.

'But I'd love to come over for dinner one night before I go back to Dubai.'

'Tomorrow then,' I said, 'There's a new recipe I've been meaning to try out, asparagus and wild mushroom risotto.'

She smiled. 'That sounds delicious.'

We said our goodbyes and she cuddled Digby again.

I said to the dog as we snuggled up on the sofa later, 'There's method in my madness, Digby.' He licked my nose. I think he understood.

Formal Night

She sweeps down the red carpet into the casino
this ordinary woman.
Transformed for a while in her glittering black gown
hair pinned high with jewelled clips,
real enough
if you don't get too close.
She could be royalty
or a film star
on the arm of her husband
unrecognizable in his tuxedo and bow tie
imagining he is Bond.
They stand by the roulette table and watch
self conscious in their naivety
while the ship ploughs on into the deep black night.

Actors

'Is that a tear rolling down your cheek, birthday girl?'

Michael leans over and takes my hand. The ending of the play is unexpectedly tender and I try to blink back the tears that are threatening to become embarrassing.

A cloudburst of glitter rains down on the young leading lady as she takes her bow, centre stage. The rest of the cast join hands and bow low, again and again. The audience clap and cheer, unwilling to let them go. Eventually the curtain descends and the applause dies away.

Michael smiles and takes my hand. 'Come on you old softy.'

We shuffle along between the seats, out of the auditorium and down to the bar for a drink. What a great birthday treat this has been. Dinner at Juno's, then on to the theatre with good seats in the centre of the third row.

We find a table in the corner and watch as the cast join the drinkers at the bar. People are pushing through the crush, eager to shake their hands and congratulate them on the success of the play. It must be great being an actor, especially on a night like this. I feel relaxed and happy, content with my lot. I smile at Michael and revel in the cosy feeling. I could stay here in this lovely atmosphere until the bar staff throw us out, but we must get back home, our teenage daughter is alone.

Reluctantly we say our goodbyes and step out into the frosty winter's night. The stars are clear and unusually bright. Rings of colour wrap the full moon, heralding the snow that is forecast for the North of England. I shiver at the prospect and wrap my cashmere scarf tighter round my neck.

Without warning, the figure of a man looms out of the darkness into the bright lights beaming from the theatre doorway.

'Can you tell me where the night shelter is?'

The words come in a rush, like his steps, but his voice is small and without strength. His whiskery face is pallid and thin, his eyes watery and staring. The unfashionable brown tweed coat is buttoned up to the neck, the collar turned up against the cold. He carries a package in his gloveless hands, just a small one wrapped in the yellow plastic of the local supermarket. He doesn't seem to be drunk, or drugged, or even distressed. He just looks ... empty.

My heart steadies to a normal beat and I try to remember where I've seen groups of unshaven, wild haired men, and sometimes the odd woman, sitting on the steps of a disused church, talking, or arguing amongst themselves, drinking from bottles and cans. I look back into those desolate eyes and point up the hill.

'I think you'll find it's up there a little way.'

He nods, 'Thanks.' And he strides off into the

night, stiff and straight, clutching his small yellow parcel. He looks frozen.

I take Michael's arm and we walk in silence to the car park. Saturday night clubbers, boys in designer shirts and girls in mini skirts, oblivious to the cold, march along the pavement, arms around each other, singing and laughing. They look so carefree.

We reach the darkness of the car park.

'I'll drive,' I say, and we sit in the car for a moment, the silence heavy between us.

Michael breaks the silence. 'Poor bugger.'

My smug feeling of wellbeing has gone, evaporated into the cold night air. There is a two sided conversation going on inside my head.

'Go back and find the man with the staring eyes. Take him home. Give him a hot meal and a warm bed. Find out ... why?'

'But what if he's a rapist, or a murderer on the run? What of our teenage daughter at home? Will she be safe? Will any of us be safe?'

'Just do it, this man is a fellow human being, deep in some sort of personal hell.'

'But what about the nauseating stench of dirty clothes and bad breath from un-cared for *teeth?'*

I switch on the ignition and the noise of the engine shatters the silence. I put the car into gear and drive away from the city centre streets. The heater blasts warmth, and Michael fiddles with the radio. I drive automatically through the dark country lanes with the man still at the forefront of my mind, blocking out all other thoughts, until the crunch of gravel and the glare of security lights jolts me back to the present. Laura opens the front door and I wrap my arms around her, hugging her tightly, breathing in the clean laundered smell of her pyjamas and newly shampooed hair. She wriggles out of my grip.

'What's up with you?'

'Nothing love, just glad to see you.'

I climb the stairs to my bedroom and kick off my boots, feeling the thick pile of the carpet between my toes. I peel of my clothes and step into the shower. The hot jets of water beat down on my shoulders and I close my eyes, trying desperately to forget those other, staring ones. I step out and dry myself on a fluffy white towel and slip between the crisp clean sheets of my comfortable bed. I turn on my side and feel Michael climbing in beside me. He holds me gently and the sound of his breathing calms me. Lying here, awake in the darkness we say nothing, but each of us knows what the other is thinking, the way couples often do.

Scottie

Scottie sits on the back of the sofa
and waits.
There's a bird on the tree outside the window.
He likes to chase birds.
When his master comes home
he'll take Scottie for a walk.
He'd love a walk
he hasn't been on many lately.

It's too warm in the living room
the fire's too big and hot
for a little dog like Scottie.
He jumps down
and chases an imaginary bird round the Christmas tree ...
It's so quiet.

Scottie's mistress picks him up
and buries her face in his curly coat.
Scottie wriggles out of her arms and runs back to the sofa.
The bird is still sitting there on the branch
snowflakes swirling round it.
One day soon his master will come walking up the garden path
all he has to do is wait.
Scottie feels sure.

Are You Listening Bernard?

It's been such a quiet Christmas without you. We went to Cheryl's on Christmas Day, Scottie and me. I couldn't face cooking Christmas dinner, not without you interfering like you always did. Every one tried to be terribly bright but the empty chair was there just the same. Emily couldn't get her head round the fact that grandad wasn't there. Where was he? It's a lot to take in when you're only three.

John has taken Scottie today. I asked if he'd have him for keeps, but he said he'd have to ask Becky. It doesn't sound too promising to me because I know she doesn't like dogs. Too house proud for her own good that girl.

It breaks my heart to see Scottie sitting on the back of the sofa day after day, waiting for you to come home. He's so full of trust, always was your dog and he just doesn't understand it.

I spoke to a bereavement councillor at the health centre the other day. The doctor said it might help to talk to someone who wasn't family. I don't know that it did though, she looked about eighteen. I suppose she must have been older. She looked like she'd never lost her car keys let alone a loved one, what would she know about it. Anyway she said that grief affects you in three ways. First there's sadness, then comes anger and then comes guilt.

Well, of course I'm sad, how can I not be? I've

lost my best friend. And yes, I am angry, bloody angry that you didn't stick to the diet the doctor gave you, and angry that you didn't cut down on the whisky and take more exercise and most angry because you've gone and left me because here I am, up on the Barrow after dark all on my own. Now I'm blubbering and I can't find my handkerchief, and it's snowing like blazes, swirling and swirling and I can't see a yard in front of me. And I suppose I do feel guilty … guilty at still being here when it was you who held our family together for so long … working so hard to keep a nice roof over our heads. All you wanted was a quiet life, a good meal at the end of the day and a whisky in front of the tele.'

Whoops! My feet are sinking into the snow, it's so deep it's coming over the top of my boots. Scottie wouldn't have been able to walk in this, his little legs are too short. Aah …

The snow's stopped falling and the stars have come out. There's a big full moon and it looks as light as day. I can see my footsteps behind me … there's no-one here but me and I'm staggering a bit … *We Three Kings of Orient are. Bearing gifts we trav …* Never could hold a tune. Can you see the trees at the bottom of the hill, Bernard? Is it my imagination or are they full of lights … colours … red … blue … twinkling … gifts … I think I'm exceptionally drunk, well, I drank nearly a bottle of whisky before I came out, what? You're surprised because I don't like whisky. But I'm lovely and numb now, and the pills the doctor gave me are making me feel quite happy. I emptied the whole packet, popped them out of their little bubbles, pop ... pop ... pop ... Monday ... Tuesday ... Wednes ... Feel much better now. I'm going to sit under that tree over there and look down at the lights of the town and then I'm going to go to sleep. Fast, fast asleep. Because I'm so tired, Bernard, and because I can't face it all without you, sweetheart.

Meeting Father Christmas

Pete crept down the dark streets lit only by the new LED lamps that gave out almost no light unless you were directly under them. He pulled his black, beanie hat down further over his ears and his scarf further up round his face. It was bloomin' cold tonight, mind you it was Christmas Eve.

Danny in 'the scrubs' had told him what a good night it was for breaking and entering. 'Rich pickings,' he said. 'All the presents round the tree and the parents out cold full of festive Bailey's and Gordon's gin.'

Only trouble were the pets, dogs could be a nuisance. 'Look for signs,' he said. Closed gates were evidently a big clue.

This house looked a good one. Nice large detached, pristine garden, open gates, no beware of the dog signs, and well away from the nearest street light.

Pete quickly looked around, then darted into the drive and sprinted round the back of the house. He could see by the light of the moon that the kitchen window was open just a little. 'Careless,' he muttered under his breath. Then he saw the reason for it. The turkey had been cooked and left on the windowsill to cool, and mum maybe in her gin and tonic haze had forgotten all about it.

Betty had done that one Christmas and next

door's cat got in and ate most of one breast. They kept schtum though and cut the chewed bits off and nobody went down with food poisoning.

Pete took a long slim bar from his bag and slipped it through the crack in the window frame lifting the catch. The window swung out and in seconds he was on the window ledge, through the window and dropping down to the smooth tiled floor. He switched on his torch and swung it around. Nice gaff, some lolly here that's for sure.

He crept silently through the kitchen into the hallway and listened. Not a sound. He carried on through double doors into a large lounge. In front of the floor to ceiling windows was a huge Christmas tree. What a beauty, what would his Sharon give for that. There was hardly space in their small sitting room for the old silver one that came out of the loft every year.

This one was laden with baubles and tinsel, but tastefully done he could see that. He would have liked to have congratulated them and was tempted just for a second to switch on the fairy lights. Then he pulled himself together. He could hear Danny's advice in his head. Concentrate on what's round the bottom of the tree. That's what he was here for after all. Most of the presents were wrapped, that was a nuisance, but there was a child's bike, a computer, and a train set laid out on the carpet ready for a quick start in the morning. He heard a sound behind him and whipped round. There, just behind him was a little girl, her eyes wide and startled. She was clutching her teddy tightly in her arms.

He stared at her, what in heaven's name was he to do now.

'Hello,' she whispered.

'Hello,' he whispered back.

'Have you brought me a bike?'

'What?' and then he twigged. 'Of course, it's what you asked for, and it's pink, I thought you'd like pink.' He shone the torch over it.

She jumped up and down with excitement and he put his fingers to his lips. 'Shhhh, we don't want to wake any one.'

I'm Abbie, and I know who you are, but you don't look like I thought you'd look. You're a lot thinner than your pictures and you haven't got a white beard.'

'Well, I've been away for a while and the food was rubbish so I've lost a bit of weight.'

Pete started to sweat. This was crazy, any minute dad was going to come down those stairs and he'd be banged up again before you could say brussel sprouts.

'Well, Abbie, it's lovely to talk to you but I must be off, I've a lot to do tonight.'

The little girl nodded. 'I quite understand, but don't forget your mince pie and the carrot for Rudolf. She ran over to the window. I can't see him anywhere.'

'Oh, I'm on my electric sleigh tonight. It gets me around a bit quicker than the reindeers.'

'Ok. Bye then,' and she turned and stomped off up the stairs. Then she turned and stomped down again. He could see her big smile in the moonlight. 'Thank you Father Christmas.'

His heart was thumping. Get out of here said a warning voice in his ear. It was his dad, long since gone but in touch now and then. He moved swiftly to the kitchen window and vaulted out onto the patio. He lifted the turkey back onto the window sill and pulled the window closed. Then he ran as if the devil himself were after him.

*

Christmas morning, Abbie sat with Freddie on the carpet opening presents in front of the Christmas tree.

'I met Father Christmas last night mummy when he brought our presents.'

Mummy carried on peeling parsnips. 'Did you, darling, that's really nice. I notice he hasn't eaten his mince pie.'

'That's because he's been on a diet like you. He's a lot thinner now, and he's been on holiday but he didn't like the hotel he stayed at, the food was rubbish.'

Abbie's mum put the parsnips in the pan. 'Oh, lovely, well, I hope you wished him Merry

Christmas from all of us.'

'No I forgot. I will do when I see him again, my new dolly is called Charlotte.'

'Lovely,' said mummy, and Abbie began to change Charlotte's dress and mummy began to whip the cream for the trifle.

Lucia Kenny

Lucia originally came from Ireland and many of her inspirations have come from her childhood experiences there.

She is the newest of the Bare Writers and finds being with the group most stimulating, and inspiring.

She loves the outdoor life and is a keen photographer, but her first love is writing.

Missing You

He's gone! I was beginning to feel the loneliness. It seemed only minutes since he was standing holding my hand. If only time stood still. I had to get over it. Keep busy, I was told. I picked up his jumper, held it close and inhaled. Those familiar smells hit my heart sorely. I must pull myself together, I wasn't the only woman who had to go through this separation. It won't always feel like this, they had said.

Later I sat sipping a cup of coffee and listening to the radio. A somewhat plaintive song rang out *how I miss you.* It was too much, I flicked the switch off. Aimlessly I wandered about the house picking up Jack's clothes, and thought, if he was here now I'd be shouting at him for being so untidy. How I wish I could do just that.

I kept looking at the clock. 'What will I do now?' I said to myself. Then the phone rang, it was Kathy checking how I was coping. 'Fine,' I lied. I didn't want to tell her I was darn right miserable. She'd only come rushing round full of sympathy, and that wasn't what I needed right now. I was already indulging myself in sympathy. I needed to be strong, stand on my own two feet, not collapse in a heap just because Jack wasn't here. I wanted out of this abyss. I needed to know I could fill the void.

I decided fresh air and a bit of shopping would lift my spirits. So I took myself off to see what the latest fashion had to offer. It was a good idea, it stopped me thinking about him for a short while. Then I went to the local supermarket. Have to buy some food, keep my strength up, I thought.

As I was loading up the shopping I saw my friend Sally with her little boy.

'Hello there,' she shouts. 'How's it going? You'll be feeling a bit odd without Jack, but it won't always feel like this. In a while, you'll enjoy the freedom.'

I didn't believe her. How can a person be so close to another and enjoy freedom when they are not around? She hadn't experienced it— well, not yet.

'You'll be okay,' she said touching my hand. I couldn't stop the tears, especially when I caught the two brown eyes of her three-year-old son staring at me in bewilderment.

By the time I got home and unpacked my shopping I was both astonished and delighted to know it was ten minutes to three. My heart leapt for joy. I grabbed the car keys and dashed to pick up Jack. I had got through my son's first day at school. I would survive!

Another Season

The summer's warmth has just slipped by
I sit beneath the weakening sun.

A cool breeze caresses my face,
a new season is almost here.

The garden has started to turn golden,
yet some foliage hangs on to life.

A display of colour from the retreating season
shows many flowers can endure the change.

I watch leaves fall gently to the ground,
like golden snowflakes they lie on the lawn.

In the distance I hear a clock chime,
the sun has already moved on.

A chilly wind blows around me,
another reminder of the season to come.

Like every season the autumn will bring beauty,
it is the change that holds the alluring mystery.

Whatever the season each one will come,
and with it comes its unique splendour.

A Different Way of Life

I was halfway round my tour in Yorkshire where I had seen some beautiful villages and met many friendly people. On one occasion I was walking along on a quiet road very much at peace with myself when I spotted in the distance a group of people by the roadside. As I drew nearer I saw on the grass verge several caged birds, geese, ducks, hens, all squawking noisily. I felt sympathy for them they didn't look overfed. And yet I knew once they had produced what eggs they could, they would certainly end up on a dinner plate—they definitely weren't pets!

I was a few hundred metres away when I saw three battered caravans which must have been the people's living quarters, one had the door open, I caught a glimpse inside. Newspapers were strewn on the floor some crumpled up making the floor a convenient waste bin. Many pots and pans sat on surfaces, and a broken handle dangled from a cupboard door. All this was guarded by a mangy cat sitting at the entrance. It hissed a warning as I passed.

When I came alongside the camp I saw an elderly woman sitting in an armchair. She had white waist-length hair, and a wrinkled walnut face battered by years of being in the elements. She sat like a queen, her hands resting on the arms of a chair more suited for a living room than outdoors. She did not move. She sat in a trance-like state looking up to something in the sky. She reminded me of Miss Havisham, a Dickensian character. The woman looked as if she was sitting waiting—for what I did not know.

Two men protectively walked around her, one had a cigarette in his mouth. He wore a flat cap low on his head. He watched me approach. My heart was pounding as I saw his unfriendly glare just visible from beneath his cap. He stamped out his cigarette-end and gave me another intimidating look. It occurred to me I was many miles from anywhere and wondered, what if I should encounter trouble? But I thought, just because these people choose to live differently, that didn't make them a wild tribe. Though, huddled together in this isolated spot it reminded of the Brigantes, an ancient tribe I had recently read about who had come to Yorkshire in pre-Roman times. Could they have been descendants? I wondered! It made me feel uneasy.

I greeted them with a smile. I got somewhere between a smirk and a grimace as a response from one of the men. I stared ahead, but the inquisitive side of me was stronger than my fear, and as I'd never been this close to a strange set of people, I wanted to file this scene in my memory. I turned my head and saw two children playing, and when they saw me they ran and clung to a woman, who I presumed was their mother. The children had a haunted look, like a deer in the forest when it sees danger approach, it stops, stares and runs off.

Then I saw another woman sitting on the ground crossed legged with the palms of her hands facing upwards. I could see her fingernails were very long and dirty. Her hair was white tied back from her face, and she too sat staring into space with not a flicker of recognition of anything around her. She appeared to be even older than Miss Havisham with an ancient face the colour of a coconut, and a skeleton-like body.

I wanted to get away from this place quickly, it was all I could do to stop myself breaking into a run, but I didn't want to show I was afraid. Then suddenly, I was startled by about six or eight very angry dogs standing on their hind legs barking ferociously. They stood baring their teeth trying desperately to charge at me. Fortunately, they were tied up with chains, but I wasn't sure the fence that they were attached to would hold them. I was sure they were hungry and would have torn me to pieces if they could have got free.

When I had gone far enough to be able to relax, I pondered the situation of these people, asking myself, how do they make a living? Do they always have enough food and clothing? I felt for them.

It made me cast my mind back to when as a child and living in the countryside in Ireland, people would come to the door selling posies which my mother bought, and she would also give them food. They looked so desperately poor, like the ones I'd just passed.

The scene I had just witnessed was a complete contrast to the affluent villages I had seen on my walking trip, but I thought, perhaps these people were happy living in their chosen environment, at least there, they were free spirits.

The Hill-Billies

Jed Jackson and Ellie Mae had been living on their ranch since the day they married. Fifty years they'd been self-sufficient and survived off their land.

The few neighbours they had, accepted a generous offer from the railway company in exchange for their land. Most had moved to Yellow Creek their nearest town. The company had plans to build a railroad across the area, but however, there was only one obstacle—Jed and Ellie Mae would not budge.

'No railroad is gonna run over ma property. This is our land, ain't nobody gonna push me and my Ellie Mae off it.'

Jed and Ellie Mae weren't too sure what a railroad was. They'd heard from other folk that it was a large engine which could puff out steam, and move across land carrying many passengers. They were God-fearing people and Jed had said,

'God has given us animals to help us survive, and ma horse can take us anywhere. We don't need no great lump of iron to take us places we wanna go.'

On the day the railroad company representatives had come, Jed stood with his pitchfork in his hand poking and threatening it towards the two men. He said if they dared move one step closer they would end up on the wrong side of his fork. The company didn't know what to do to encourage them to sell, so they waited, biding their time.

Then Jed became seriously ill and the doctor was sent for, he had said Jed needed to go to a hospital, but was too ill to make the journey. Ellie Mae was distraught. She realised how isolated they were from other folk.

Jed was deteriorating fast, his breathing laborious and his face deathly pale. Ellie Mae was sitting by his bedside when in a barely audible voice, he whispered,

'Ellie Mae, you won't cope out here on your own. You'd better sell up.'

'I ain't goin anywhere without you. You'll be around to take care of things. You said you would!'

'But things may not work out. Promise me you'll move? Ellie, promise me?' he pleaded.

She reached over and stroked his damp brow, and promised she'd move into town. In her heart, she wasn't sure what she'd do. All their lives Jed had made all the decisions, but she supposed she'd have to keep her promise. Anxiously she fiddled with her brooch and recalled the day Jed had surprised her with this gift. It was contrary to his nature to buy anything so grand, but he'd bought it to make reparation for shouting at her and making her cry. Now her tears were of a different nature, she'd give anything to have him well again and holler at her.

Ellie Mae thought on Jed's words. She'd have to make a decision. If she was left on her own, how would she manage out here on the ranch? She knew the answer - she couldn't. She'd have to sell and move into Yellow Creek where her friends and neighbours had moved to.

Many months later Ellie Mae stood on her porch in Yellow Creek and watched the folk walk up and down the muddy dirt track in the street. She was happy she'd moved. She had fewer jobs to do about the house which left her more time to herself, and the food store had just about everything she wanted. However not all around her was happy, as she heard a voice call from behind her.

'What you doin out there? Come in and close that door. Can't get any peace in this darn place. Shouldn't have kept that promise. Bringing me to this Godforsaken hole.'

The Odd Couple

He stood small podgy and round,
she stood highest from the ground.
His thick arms hung like two blocks of wood,
like shafts of a brush hers dangled where she stood.

When he spoke his tone was light and sweet,
while her voice roared out loud and deep.
He loved to dance with his twinkle-toed feet,
watching the wrestling was her weekly treat.

His excitement was raised by betting on horses,
she fretted if her voice developed hoarseness.
A pie and pint he liked to savour,
dinner at the Ritz she did favour.

On Friday afternoon they had lunch in the park,
and sat there together until it was dark.
He ate his pie and not a word did they speak,
until he had finished then he kissed her cheek.

For thirty years their romance did grow,
but never a gold ring was to bestow.
Their characters were so far apart,
both different planets of the heart.

Little endearments occurred in their dreams,
but they still stuck together - odd as it seems.

What they had in common no one knew,
perhaps their oddities gives us a clue.

'What is that bloody picture doing on that wall?' growled Jack.

'It reminds me of you dear? That's why I painted it,' said his wife with a twinkle in her eye.

'How the hell can it remind you of me? Do I look like a tree or a bloody elephant? Doesn't say much for me. Eh?'

Jack studied the picture, he couldn't for the life of him see why a baby elephant on a tree could relate to him. 'Stupid fool,' he mumbled.

Tony their son came home from work, he added to the insult.

'What the hell is that?'

'Just a picture your mum decided reminded her of me.'

'Of you?' Tony burst into fits of laughter. 'I never thought of you as a baby elephant Dad. Clumsy! Yes.'

'Less of your cheek boy. You're not too old to get a clip round the ear.'

'Sorry, Dad. Only joking.'

What have I started? thought Molly. But she wasn't taking the picture down. It did really symbolise what Jack meant to her, though she didn't expect him to understand.

So the picture stayed and each night Jack turned the picture to face the wall and each morning

Molly turned it back again. It was just something they couldn't agree about, but they were not going to get into an argument over it, and so they learned to live with an uncompromising situation.

It was about one year later Tony and his mum had just come from the crematorium. Tony helped his mother into the chair and pushed a drink into her hand.

'Get that down you Mum.'

Sighing Tony's mum said, 'I don't know what I'll do without your Dad.'

Staring at the picture of the elephant tree Tony said, 'Aye, we'll all miss him. But tell me, Mum. How come this picture reminded you of Dad? I mean an elephant and a tree I can't get the connection'

He'd asked her many times before, but she'd laughed it off and never gave him a satisfactory reply.

'Well, son it's like this. There are two ways of looking at the tree and the elephant in relation to your Dad. A tree has many appearances, this one is strong unadorned, rough, no niceties about it, that is one side to your Dad, and you could say the same about an elephant. It can be frightening yet, it can be tamed to suit man's needs, then it becomes like a gentle giant.

Another side of the tree is that it produces delicate leaves, I compare those leaves with the love your father had for me. It flourished, and when leaves fall and die, more grow again. But just as leaves are prolific so was his love. And like his love, the tree reproduces bigger and stronger leaves as it matures.'

Tony looked at the picture it always made him laugh, but now he saw something deeper, something beautiful. 'Did you ever tell him?'

'No son. Perhaps I should have, but knowing your Dad he wouldn't have handled the sentimentality very well. He'd probably have said, it was a load of twaddle.'

'And how on earth do you get a soft side of an elephant?' Tony asked.

'Ah well, that might appear more difficult. But your Dad was not the most gentle person in the world, graceless in fact. But he cared for you and me just like a baby. That's why I made it a baby elephant. So there you have it son.'

Tony put his arms around his mother. 'Thanks for telling me.' Then laughing he said, 'But you know what? I'm still going to turn the picture to face the wall each night.'

'I'd like that son. I'd really like that.'

Broken Forest

The wind ripped through the forest
like a banshee wailing
devastating everything before it.
Broken limbs lay strewn on the ground.

When the tempest became calm
a thick mist fell like a shroud
covering the ground
as if protecting the fallen.

Fractured trees stretch out on the forest floor,
some roots defiantly cling to the earth
clutching at life to regenerate
and give birth to saplings.

Even the lost souls on the ground
will decompose
and give back to earth what they took
and so another cycle begins.

Allan Bolton

Allan joined Bare Writers in 2015, keen to write creatively after a career of fact-based writing which included a book and numerous articles.

He now draws on a lifelong love of reading, from history, sport, popular music and from walking the hills and landscapes of our national trails.

'Take it from me, Mike. Going about on the railways is simply awful these days. Overcrowded, noisy, not even civilised. The only way to make it half-bearable is to go first-class.'

Monica's response to Mike's dewy-eyed announcement of his plan to reconnect with fondly-remembered rail journeys in his younger days was characteristically definitive. Monica travelled worldwide for work, knew what she was talking about. Mike, whose job included approving her expenses, excused her for being a bit of a precious prima donna of the skies, roads and rails. Monica had to be rested, alert and persuasive at conventions throughout south-east Asia; a few pricey flights and comfortable trains were a sensible investment in keeping the business model rolling.

Mike's pre-retirement plans were about market intelligence, networking and public relations – unquantifiable benefits compared with the hundreds of thousands which Monica helped harvest. A bit of discomfort was nothing to him, a delight compared with his increasing horror of congested roads and confusing car parks.

His first experience of 'going about on the railways' held a surprise. Boarding a frequently-stopping service bound for Manchester Piccadilly, Mike was intrigued to notice that on every seat was a business card. A loyalty bonus, special offer, or some other imaginative marketing ploy, he imagined. But no. Printed boldly was 'Sorry we made you late. . . Claim back between 50% and 100% of the price of your ticket'. The service was on time. This couldn't be right. To Mike it was negative thinking on a grand scale, a public relations failure of a kind which training videos illustrated. The actual deficiency was in the nature of the carriage: tatty old seats, filthy windows, littered floors. As he got up to drop a sandwich wrapper into a bin like a letter box, his eye was caught by a notice overhead: 'Hi, my name is carriage 57118. I always try to look my best.' Yes, rail travel had changed a lot.

Modernisation was going on in some places. On Mike's evening ride home from work, he stepped into sleek new air conditioned carriages, seats set out to optimise capacity, yet allowing decent amounts of personal space. His nostrils were assailed by odours emanating from KFC wrappers on the laps of two spotty, noisy teenagers. Moving swiftly into the next coach, he was happy to sit where only one other passenger was visible. 'Welcome to the Bradford Forster Square train. The next stop is Frizinghall,' blared the computerised voice.

'Oh, is that so? Well, well. And I'm going to Ilkley. This is what you get with privatised railways. And when I get there, I still have to get a bus, to Otley, the largest town in Yorkshire *without a railway station*.'

Mike heard this frustrated grumble with a sense of detached amusement, even with recognition, for last week he had heard those very same words from the very same voice. Whereas then the speaker was hidden by a crowd of commuters, tonight his identity was revealed, if only partially through two untidy tufts of grey hair and the back of a head visible between seats two rows in front. The speaker seemed content to address what he must have assumed was an empty coach.

Malfunctioning high tech equipment was a legend on this line, albeit most travellers were delighted with the underlying improvements. The regular conductors' witty asides could put Mike into a good mood for a whole morning. As the train slowed for its approach to the city terminus, a chatty announcement came: 'Ladies and gentlemen, you may be aware that last week-end automatic ticket barriers were installed. There are still some teething problems which might hold you up. The machines are made by a company called Scheidt and Bachmann. We think that Mr Bachmann had a day off.'

A long career had made a reputation for Mike amongst his counterparts, one of whom invited him to act briefly as consultant. He would enjoy a day out providing advice to a newer organisation in a city on the South coast. 'Get a flight, man, for Heaven's sake,' were Monica's words. But for Mike, the prospect of a leisurely journey without holding lounges, passports and security checks was much more appealing. His meetings would be short enough to fit in a return journey and still be home by 9 p.m. OK, there'd be three changes of train, but somehow that didn't register with Mike.

The final meeting wound to a close, Mike having endorsed what was happening at the southern organisation and encouraged more confident further progress. The host expressed his appreciation of Mike's contribution: '… good to know that we're on the right lines … means a lot … from someone at a *proper* institution.' Those final words, no doubt meant light-heartedly on a Friday afternoon, drew frowns and sighs from several of his colleagues around the table.

The journey home began smoothly, just as the morning's outward journey had been throughout. The last of the trains required to complete the five hour return had delivered most of its passengers to the platforms of Birmingham, Crewe, Warrington, Wigan. North of Wigan meant almost home. Without earlier warning, an announcement came that owing to week-end track improvement works, this train would terminate at Preston. In fact, it wouldn't even make it to Preston: it would stop at somewhere called Euxton Balshaw Lane. A replacement bus would take passengers to Preston.

Mike knew already that improvements

normally meant disruption and inconvenience. 'More bloody improvements,' he thought.

Ten tired but tolerant passengers quietly stepped down at Euxton Balshaw Lane to find, nothing; a small ill-lit location not well endowed with tarmac roads. Dusk was fading into dark under leafy boughs hanging over a stony path which connected the station to a distant outside world. Within five minutes, powerful headlights transformed the scene from the only road. Within half an hour the bus driver drew up outside Preston station with the words, 'Here we are. Sorry for the hold-up. Job done!'

For three of them travelling beyond Preston, it was not job done. When a railway official peered through the gloom of 10 p.m. Mike asked him how they could reach Lancaster. 'Just take any of these taxis. The cost's covered.' The two young ladies shivering and looking apprehensive were heading in the same destination, for Morecambe for a wedding the following day they said. As the taxi took them beyond junction 32 and began the 13 miles unlit stretch to the next junction, the hills of Bowland loomed as if with sinister intent to gobble up the highway and everything on it. The paler of the girls gazed with foreboding in her shaky voice. 'I never realised it would be – so – far – North.'

The young Asian taxi driver muttered that he now didn't know where he was going so Mike offered to provide directions. Perching forward on the rear seat, he advised where to leave the motorway, how to navigate Lancaster's traffic system. The driver seemed unnerved by the lane switching and the speed of other vehicles. Mike tried to bolster his confidence. 'Keep following signs for A6 Carnforth.'

Later, the minor road that narrowed through impending trees suddenly lurched to the right prior to lurching to the left over a tiny canal bridge. The movement was too much for the pale girl. 'Please, stop. I need to get out.'

Her friend followed, uttering the useless words, 'Are you all right, mate?' but she steadied the pale one who vomited into the vegetation below the canal's supporting wall.

'Where exactly are you going?' asked Mike, when they'd clambered unsteadily back into the cab.

'Place called Hatlex Drive,' said the more coherent one. 'My aunt's house.'

Mike thought as quickly as his numbed brain allowed. 'Oh, that's not really Morecambe. It's just here down this slope on the left.' To the driver he added, 'Good news my friend. You can drop all three of us in almost the same place. I'll point your way back to Preston.'

The following Monday, Mike was back in the office where Monica was holding forth about her recent experiences in Kuala Lumpur, the cancelled flight, the unscheduled stop-over in Singapore, the 15 hour day interviewing in a humid hotel lounge. 'So, how are your railway journeys going?'

'Quite … adventurous, I'd say. I do have to admit that your assessment of modern rail travel was correct. You're usually right, aren't you?'

'Always, Mike. Always.'

from city newspaper, Richmond, Virginia, 1870

'HELP WANTED

Wanted for immediate employment: graduate of a relevant course or technical competency. No experience required. Meticulous, honest, loyal, punctual, dependable. Willing to put in long hours, lacks interest in office politics or gossip. Duties include repetitive activities, detailed observation and organization. Competitive salary with benefits. Write to . . .'

I sense an opportunity. In my line of business, a hunch can be a vital thing. I'm between jobs: my detective agency just crashed. Not enough clients, an expensive junior partner, a few bad debts. Above all a new and evidently successful rival company in town. This could be their work.

My name's Isaac, by the way. But I'm not giving any more details.

So, no cases to investigate, and I'm restless. There can't be many local firms keen to expand. This city is pretty much shot: attacked by the Union army, deserted as militarily indefensible by the Confederacy, on the losing side, impoverished and no longer able to use cheap slave labor, hit this year by a major flood and the collapse of the courthouse killing 60 people. Judgements from the Almighty, many citizens believe.

I need to know for sure. They recognise me in the newspaper office so I arouse no suspicion at the classified desk. I show the advert. 'We'd like to repeat this next week.'

'Sure thing. I'll just need your signature and another $10.' The clerk passes a self-carbonating pad across the desk. I let it linger long enough to scrawl an unrecognisable name and read that the previous insertion was placed by a Mr McKinnon acting for 'Swift and Sure Investigation Bureau'. That's the one.

I slide the money over the desk and the clerk gives me a receipt. Losing the cash is painful, of course: I can hardly claim expenses from S and S. I see it as a downpayment on my future.

Now I know who I'm dealing with, I craft my letter of application. I tell a good story about meeting all their requirements. I judge that mentioning my previous detecting experience will give me an advantage. I gamble that these guys won't have noticed my tiny, failing business. All their staff are blow-ins from out of state, keen to fatten their caseload with the many missing persons, displaced families and fugitive ex-soldiers hereabouts. Everyone went in fear of their lives if they fell foul of either army. The war's over, but the consequences resound.

It's the other side of Washington from here, but 11,000 men were listed as missing after the Battle of Gettysburg. Discount the many who were blown into unidentifiable pieces by cannon shells - now we know what modern warfare is like - and those deserters too traumatized or cunning to remain in the lines of fire. You're left with hundreds, maybe over a thousand, guys who've disappeared from their army, scattered and not returned to families and girls who are pining and mourning. Or not quite mourning, but clinging to a desperate fading hope that one day, their loved one will limp on to their land, collapse into their arms, resume work and so save their family from penury. More likely he'll have died in the open, a victim of outlaws, starvation or exposure. But, as long as there's hope and a little money left, there may be work for a skilled detective.

My hunch is that S and S will interview me, if only out of curiosity. I'll convey enthusiastic knowledge of the work, including the dull stuff – tracking elusive reluctant contacts, travelling incognito, keeping watch for hours in discomfort, making rigorous notes, reliably reporting back. I have visions of fruitless searches in the vastnesses of Nebraska or Wyoming, as challenged as my quarry by the harshness of the wilderness. I can create new identities – professional gambler, for example – inhabit alternative personalities. I've no interest in loose talk, except when I'm eavesdropping, or in points-scoring in an office. The only person I'll be out to cultivate is the boss.

I'll become indispensable, then make my move. In one future, I'll use what I've learned to reform my own company taking some S and S staff with me, maybe in a distant state. In another future, I'll be junior partner, eventually the boss, of S and S. In a third future, I'll diversify into a related dark, lucrative field of operations – searching out people and, to contract or otherwise, making them disappear. S and S put me out of business for now, but that's just the beginning. The past's over. S and S can disappear. They're about to find out how quickly the hunters can become the hunted.

Words on the Walkway

Thank God I decided to walk to and from work today, Martin thought. I still need to clear my head to handle this overwhelming concern, this crisis. As if that's not enough, I'm relieved to put distance between myself and the office where this afternoon's appointment went particularly badly.

His new client had proved resentful. He'd been referred by his employers in whose language Andrew's performance had 'plateaued', 'flat-lined'. Both he and Martin might suspect that this course of executive coaching was a last chance to restore the organisation's confidence in Andrew. Thinking back on their tense meeting, Martin conceded to himself that he'd failed to use several known ploys to induce the man to open up. Was Martin really any good at this new career?

Well, yes, I could be, Martin believed, but I was not as present mentally as I was physically: thinking about Sally and how to rescue our marriage overshadowed all else.

Last week, Sally had glared at him from a distance to which they were now accustomed and uttered for the third time this month, 'I – want – a – divorce.'

The first time she'd said it, it was very late and she was about to refill again her glass with the harmless-looking clear liquid she favoured. The second time, she'd terminated a contemptuous tirade about Martin's temperamental tendencies with an exasperated outburst which he'd taken as satirical humour.

The third time of uttering with her clear unblinking gaze and slow, heavy emphasis on each word, left no room for doubt.

He walked head down to shut out distractions from his major worries, oblivious to the city's mighty river as it rolled into its estuary with the North Sea. His route was a pavement with a parallel cycle-path. Just then his attention was arrested by three words spray-painted in clear white capitals on the tarmac:

ELLE
CAITLIN
COURTNEY

On the pavement, in red, were the words 'CAITLIN U R AWESOME'.

Why should these expressions, no doubt of idle teenagers, interest him? No reason. But, as he briefly broke stride, a new worry gripped him. His 14 year old elder daughter was called Elle, surely not a common name in this down-to-earth suburb. And, he thought, the way the writer had formed the letters U and R closely resembled Elle's self-conscious writing style with its tail-end flourishes of playful individuality.

So, the crisis could be more complex and threatening than he thought. He knew well his wife's directness and changes of mind; those qualities had always fascinated him and made them a complementary couple. Now Sally showed an edge of hostility that was barely hidden. She drank more, and saw friends less, than she used to. Perhaps, with his new fears about Elle, Martin could suspect that an awkward relationship with her elder daughter was undermining Sally's happiness.

Martin knew that such theories were attractive because they absolved him from blame. His mind was consumed with alternative, dark thoughts. He had become too passive, joked about his female-dominated household and ceded sole leadership to Sally. His calm manner, intended to reassure his family about his mid-life career change, was viewed as negligent and selfish. It was a cliché that he had driven Sally to drink, but that did not mean it wasn't true. His new-found worry about Elle was not fanciful: he spent less time with her than he should and it may be that Sally felt a loss of rapport with her daughter. Was her demand for a divorce a scream for overdue attention and help from him? If her demand was genuinely felt, then matters were even more serious: Sally was willing to split the family just to be rid of Martin's failing harmful influence.

With increasing doubts about his career

weakening his self-confidence, Martin knew he had to face up and repair broken relationships whilst at a disadvantage. He must also take the risk of delivering new highly unwelcome news about Elle. His words could be rehearsed no longer.

At the house, he walked in observant, to assess Sally's mood and sobriety. She soon came down the stairs with a small glass of sherry – a departure for her, he thought. 'Having a drink?' she asked.

'I'll boil up a cup of tea,' said Martin. Sally curled her lip.

Hoping to convey thoughtful reflection, he asked, 'Darling, did you really mean what you said, about divorce?'

'Yes, of course. You're not the man I married. How could I be any more clear?'

That lingering hope gone, Martin faced the challenge of understanding better Sally's state of mind, then convincing her of his continuing love, his commitment to remedying his failings, his wish to avoid separation, whilst not being dismissive of her stated desire to divorce. All that whilst taking pains to avoid another flare-up.

'I saw Bob Jackson today,' he continued. 'Remember he acted for us when we bought this house? Thought I'd sound him out, about the divorce thing.'

'What! How could you? Without asking me

or telling me. That's so *you.*'

'It was nothing formal, no commitment involved. I don't know any other solicitors. He wouldn't be able to act for both of us, obviously. He could act for you, or me.'

'To hell with either option. He's your buddy. He recruited you to his blasted cricket team which you played for till only last year.'

'Anyway, he sketched out the possible grounds for divorce. The petitioner – that'd be you – would need to evidence one of adultery, desertion, or unreasonable behaviour. Or there's separation of a length depending on whether I'd give consent.'

'You sound positively keen. Can't wait to be rid of me, eh?'

'Not at all. I don't want us to divorce. I still love you. I had to respond to what you've been saying about wanting to.'

'Separation's no good. It'd take too long. It wouldn't be adultery, though what do I know? I can relate to unreasonable behaviour. For a start, you've changed big-time. You've become a bloody pain since you switched to coaching. You used to be confident, expressive, even occasionally amusing, when you had the corporate job. Now you're brooding, silently disapproving, damn well virtuous. Every time we have a conversation, there's a misunderstanding or a row. You irritate the hell out of me when you don't just bore me senseless. I could give scores of examples.'

'Yes, you'd need to.'

'Oh, thanks for that. Damned calm and virtuous, again.'

'You could well be right. Perhaps my job does have something to do with it. In my old job I listened in order to talk, to represent, be a spokesman. Now I talk, just a little, in order to listen.'

Martin had run out of constructive things to say, so he steeled himself to tell Sally about what he saw on his walk home.

'And you think that Elle wrote that stuff? It's not even on her way between home and school, and I've never heard her mention anyone with those names - I think.'

'You must admit, Elle's an unusual name for round here.'

'Next you'll be telling me that you've Googled it and found that it's only the 43rd most common girl's name in the North East in 2004.'

'It probably is, something like that. I did worry that naming her after a supermodel might help make her into a little princess.'

'So you were right, so wise? There's nothing remotely like that about Elle. She's perfectly good, well-adjusted, especially since Emily was born.'

'We don't know what she's like outside the

home. If she's friends with a Caitlin and a Courtney, I worry. They could be a toxic trio. She's at a dangerous age, obviously.'

'What are you getting at?'

'I've never been happy about that school. She could be led astray by girls, and boys, you wouldn't approve of. Caitlin sounds Irish, Catholic and, if she's 'awesome', I dread to think how. And who'd name their daughter Courtney, presumably after a punk rock chick whose life is famous for being a car crash?'

'Martin, you are a seething pit of prejudices. The more life experience you get, the narrower your mind becomes. And the more elaborate theories you build on flimsy or non-existent evidence. That'll be another feature of your work: observe in silence, and let your imagination construct theories about what drives your clients to be as they are. Just lighten up. Start worrying when there's something to worry about. I need another drink. I'm off upstairs to clear my head.'

As soon as Sally disappeared, Martin slyly poured himself a glass of vodka. Neat, but not too much, so that Sally wouldn't notice when she next sought succour from the bottle.

After ten minutes, Martin's mobile rang.

'It's me. Sally. I know it's stupid, but I'm phoning you because it seems we can communicate better this way, out of sight. I've thought over everything and, no, I *don't* want a divorce. Tell you why: if we divorced, I'd get custody of Elle and Em. You'd be out of the picture apart from the odd weekend. Why should you go free while I have to deal with those two? I have to admit Elle's a bit of a nightmare already and I need your help to stop Em going the same way.'

'Sally, I think you're absolutely right. There's no way I want a divorce. I promise I'll try to become bearable. Please let me make things better, for all of us. Please ring off, come down, and let's talk.'

On the Ridgeway

Under canopy of chasing cloud, a following wind thrums in my ears
seven hundred feet above distant seas, rushes over these vast mid-lands,
along the ridge, its swell, sinuous curves and softness like a woman.
I, a lover, am a speck in immense space and aeons of time.

Joyful jargoning of uncounted birds drowns drone of little plane,
hum of high passenger jet,
both bullied into obscurity.

Ancient hill fort guards urban density and M4, become a place
of words and flowers to remember dear departed. Pre-Christian, now Christian-lite.

Burly Wessex wind, battled by rooks,
hurls heavy cumulus across pied sky,
aiding me north and east,
rushes and roars in tall branches.

Ancient camps called castles, places of security and refuge,
pagan redoubts that now overlook farms planted,

fenced, coppiced.
In expanse of solar panels below I see that
the Sun God is worshipped
yet on these plains of middle England.

Gill Wistowsky

Gill grew up among the 'Dark satanic mills' and coalfields of South Yorkshire, moving to the beautiful Morecambe Bay area in 2013. Her inspiration comes from anywhere and everywhere, but it is, perhaps, the pit spoil-heaps and scarred urban landscapes of her childhood that take her imagination to the strange and often dark places she explores in her writing.

Three Wishes

He was a small man with a shiny bald head and large, protuberant eyes. He stopped me in the middle of a busy street filled with early morning shoppers. Normally I just smile and walk on; the town centre always has its share of 'chuggers' waiting to pounce on the unwary. But something about the man stopped me in my tracks. Maybe it was his smart appearance amongst the casually dressed shoppers, but I think it's just that he managed to make eye-contact so I found myself stopping, at the same time telling myself I wasn't going to be talked into anything. I already make a contribution to charity, I would tell him, smiling before walking away.

'Hello,' he said in a calm, disarmingly warm and gentle voice 'would you like me to grant you three wishes?' Well, what could you say to a question like that? It was certainly a new approach! I wondered what he was selling - he didn't have the usual charity badge - as I laughingly answered, 'one would be enough.'

'Oh dear, I'm sorry,' he replied 'it doesn't work like that. I'm afraid it has to be three, or none at all.' He stood there, watching me expectantly as I tried to think of something to say in response. His manner was diffident, unhurried among the bustle, but his eyes were deep and penetrating as they gazed into mine and I was completely disarmed. The street around me seemed to recede, become unreal, the people hurrying by like shadows. I shook myself inwardly, like a dog shedding water, to try and break the spell. Was I being hypnotised by those eyes?

I found myself saying, 'OK, I'll take the three wishes, but I'm not selling my soul for them or anything like that. And I'm not buying anything or agreeing to give away half my income, or any of it.' What an absurd thing to say I thought as soon as the words came out of my mouth, so I shrugged and laughed a little, trying to sound light-hearted. But I'd begun to feel a deep sense of unease which was immediately dispelled by his next words.

'The wishes are completely free and without obligation. They can be anything at all from the realms of the possible or beyond.' His smile lit up the street and his teeth glowed white in the gloom of the January day. Again, I had the feeling that the people around me were unreal; only this strange man and myself existed, and anything was possible, anything I wished for ...

I began to imagine the world of possibilities before me as he continued, 'but think carefully before you choose, and choose well. And you must decide before you take another step.'

Suddenly I found myself rooted to the spot, unable to move a muscle. The world of possibilities had become a universe of despair. What could someone wish for when given that choice? I looked again into his eyes and saw only darkness and a despair that reflected my own. I realised something else then, his stillness was a deliberate stance to avoid moving his feet. 'You have the burden now,' he said. 'You must choose, say your wishes out loud, or pass them on to another soul.' With that, he smiled a smile of deep sadness, turned and walked away.

That was many hours ago and I haven't moved a step. It's getting darker and there's a chill in the air, but I don't feel the cold. I don't feel anything beyond the burden of choice. The people are still rushing by, but there are fewer of them now and my mind is awash with choices: world peace, an end to hunger, an end to illness and disease; but what would be the unforeseen consequences of any of these options? I see an older man approaching and decide to accost him before he passes. I touch him gently on his arm and gaze into his eyes. 'Hello, would you like me to grant you three wishes?'

Fairy Tale

There's always a Wolf
sleek and smiling, offering forbidden
thrills. His deadly grin, those teeth,
sharp as daggers, will rip out your heart
then eat you up till nothing's left
but bloody bones.

You were Red Riding Hood
skipping through the wood
carrying your basket of treats.
But you didn't heed your mother's warning
not to stray from the path.
You saw a flash of crimson fur
and followed where it led.
You were lost.

Then the Woodcutter came and found you,
but he cut off your head, instead
and left you for dead.
Now the Wolf and the Woodcutter
are making their own story
about how Red Riding Hood
came with her basket of tricks
and stole the heart of the wolf
and kept it in her trinket box,
till the woodcutter

came with his axe
and set it free.

Dav's Story

My name is Dav and I'm eleven summers old. I live with my Ma and Da and my sister Bee. Bee is smaller than me so I have to look after her when we go out scavenging, but I don't mind. She's quick and her eyes are sharp and we find lots of useful things. Because I'm bigger and stronger than Bee I can lift things that she can't and put them in the cart. We make a good team, even though there are only two of us. Ma had other kids but they all sickened and died. There are six stone mounds at the back of our house, one for each of the dead babbies, and sometimes Ma goes out there and cries, quietly. Bee and I don't disturb her then, but when she comes back to us she's cheerful again for a while.

Sometimes she tells us stories about the Old Times. We don't think the stories are true, but we love to listen to them anyway, because Ma sounds so happy when she's telling us about the tall buildings with real glass windows, where lots of people lived all crowded together. They travelled around in shiny metal machines on wheels and sometimes in machines that flew like birds, but much bigger, carrying hundreds of people. I don't believe in machines that fly, but maybe some of the other stuff is true.

Once I journeyed with Da to a place where lots of buildings stood with broken walls and roofs.

They looked as if people had lived there, but they'd all gone away. Ma says only ghosts live there now, and Da gives her a funny look, like he wants to say something about the thing that happened while we were there. But he never has, so I haven't either.

Da said there was stuff left over from the Old Times that could be useful to us, and that this was to be an Adventure and a Big Scavenger Hunt, but Bee couldn't come with us because she was too small, and Ma had to stay home with her, so it was to be just Da and me. We both had a backpack and we walked for three days, sleeping under the stars at night and pulling the cart behind us during the day. We followed the old roads where we could and I was happy to be away from home and walking with my Da, but I noticed that he was watchful and a little strung-out, like our young dog Flint when he senses something moving out in the field.

That was when I learned that we weren't alone in the wide world. Da said there were other people like us, living with their families and trying to get by, but that not all the others out there were like us and that it was better not to be seen or heard by them. So we had to be on our guard whenever we travelled away from home. I took to being watchful like Da and chattered less as we walked. I was glad that Da had told me about the Others and felt very grown-up as we pulled the cart along, keeping to the side of the road under the cover of the trees.

We eventually arrived at the place with the broken-down buildings - Da called it a town - and began to carefully make our way to the stores, creeping along quietly and making sure we knew our way back to where we'd hidden the cart. I didn't know what the stores would look like, but guessed they'd be something like the cellar where we stored our fruit and vegetables through the winter, but they were nothing like that. It turned out they were broken-down buildings too, like the houses where people had lived. Different buildings had stored different kinds of things on shelves or rails, but most of them were empty or just full of junk.

At last we found a few things we could use. There were half a dozen blankets, all new and without holes, that had been hidden under a pile of rubbish we were picking through, and with them were three pairs of boots of different sizes and a warm winter coat that was too big for me then but fits me now. Da said the boots would do for the leather if nothing else. I wished we could find something for Bee but the boots were all too big and there was nothing else. Da said the place had been ransacked and we were lucky to find the blankets and other things. I started to get tired but Da said we had to make sure we didn't leave anything useful behind, so we stacked our stuff in a neat pile and hid it behind some broken shelves, then carried on searching. We found a few other useful things and stashed everything into our backpacks. I wore the coat and Da strung the boots from his belt with the laces. They swung against him as he walked but he said it was ok and we must hurry and get back to the cart. We made our way back quickly but carefully. There was no sign of other people and I could see that Da was more relaxed now, though still watchful.

As we walked I began to notice things about the town that I hadn't seen before, like how some of the buildings had almost completely disappeared leaving big gaps open to the sky, while others around them were still standing. It made me think of Bee and the gaps in her mouth where her baby teeth had come out. Ma said we must be careful and take good care of our teeth now, as we only get one set of grown-up teeth and if we lose them they're gone forever and we'll have trouble chewing our food. I was thinking on this when I noticed a big building that was different from the others. It looked as though it had been there a long time and the others had grown up around it, like babbies clustering around their Ma. Part of the building was much higher and thinner than the rest, like a finger pointing to the sky. But the strangest thing was that some of the windows had bits of glass still in them and they glowed in the light with all the colours in the rainbow. I wondered what sort of people had lived there and was about to ask Da when the thing happened.

I heard a sound. Da and I both froze and then it came again, 'mama, mama.' Suddenly Da sprang up and rushed to a pile of rubble, disappearing behind it. I followed, more slowly, and the sound came again, together with the thump of something falling. As I got closer I saw Da with his hands around the throat of something, only not something, someone. I was scared. I wanted to run and hide but I wanted to help Da too. Then I saw the someone was a girl, a little younger than me. She looked a bit like Bee but the coat she was wearing was old and patched and her feet were bare and dirty. I called out, 'Da, Da,' but he ignored me and just kept squeezing her neck. Her tongue was sticking out of her mouth and she looked strange, then Da let go and she flopped onto the floor and was still. I didn't know what to do, but Da said, 'Come on, we've got to go, she's one of the Others.' She still seemed like a girl to me, but I looked around and saw the thing that she'd dropped. I picked it up. It was a doll that said 'mama, mama' when you turned it over. I had something to give to Bee now. She'd be really pleased.

That was two summers ago and Bee still has the doll, though it no longer says 'mama' when you turn it over. Da and I haven't been on a Big Scavenger Hunt since that time. He says there's hardly anything left that's useful now so it's not worth the journey. Ma says it doesn't matter, we can manage very well with what we make and mend and grow ourselves. So I've never seen any more of the Others, or people like us, just trying to get by.

Summer's End

That was to be the last time
she'd see the sea,
though we didn't know it then.
The sun was high in the sky, casting no shadows
as she smiled, carefree, into the camera.
I smiled too, but dutifully -
a day by the sea with mum
not really my idea of fun.

It was a last golden day in September.
I'd wanted to spend it with friends
but she, alone and in need,
said 'Wouldn't it be lovely to take a picnic
and eat it by the sea like when you were small?'
So, reluctantly, I agreed.

We'd just eaten ice-cream. I wanted to swim,
but she said she'd just paddle her feet in the briny;
she loved the feel of salt-water on her skin,
good for the rheumatism, she said,
stepping, laughing, into the swell.
Then, she just keeled over - and was dead.

Walking Away

He walks away with soft uncertain tread,
a figure tense and hunched against the cold,
with eyes fixed firmly on the road ahead
he ponders on the price of growing old.

The last of his old comrades laid to rest
with platitudes and tired empty phrases,
his thoughts go running back into the past
to seek again those lost and buried faces.

His memories of those days are sharp as stone
where yesterday is muddy, dark and dim -
he walks the world forgotten and alone,
a silent ghost amongst his living kin.

The old man feels that Death is drawing near
and welcomes his approach without demur.

Old Tom's Last Request

It's the first cold day in November and the long Indian summer at last gives way to the onset of winter. Tom shivers as he walks the mile or so to his allotment, feeling the unaccustomed chill creep under his jacket and into his bones. He's carrying a shopping bag containing an apple, a kitchen knife, his daughter's telephone number written on a pad and a bin-liner tied up with string. Inside the bin-liner are the ashes from the fire on which he burned the dog.

Tom is old and lonely and sick, and the dog was the only living creature on this earth who had any time for him. He was her god and she worshipped him with absolute devotion. And now she's dead. And soon, he will be too and no-one to miss him except his daughter, but they've never been close and she'll be relieved to see him underground; all neat and tidied away in a decent grave where she can visit and lay flowers and not have to stay too long.

The dog's name was Gertie. He and Rose would laugh and call her dirty Gertie as she was so fond of rolling in whatever muck she could find on their daily walks together. He and Rose and Gertie, they'd been a team from the day they brought Gertie home from the animal shelter and introduced her to her new home. She'd immediately laid claim to the basket in front of the fire, empty since their last dog, Lady had died months earlier. They'd never thought they'd be able to replace her but, as Rose had said, Gertie was certainly no Lady!

Tom and Rose had been married for nearly fifty years and had been looking forward to celebrating their golden wedding with a cruise around the Mediterranean. They'd never been on a cruise ship before but Rose had been looking forward to it so much he'd been caught up in her enthusiasm despite his own misgivings. He'd imagined the types of people who went in for that kind of thing as snobbish, but Rose had assured him that it wasn't at all like that these days, and that all kinds of people went in for cruise holidays. Everything was laid on for you and there was the chance to visit lots of different places. She'd started buying new clothes for them both in anticipation, and had been busy planning what they would see in the places they visited.

Gertie was to stay with Tom's neighbour at the allotments, Arthur and his missus. Arthur and Jen loved dogs but Jen wasn't up to looking after one full-time these days, so Gertie had become a kind of surrogate pet. She'd miss them while they were away, but Tom knew she'd be spoilt to death by Arthur and Jen. Probably wouldn't want to come home, he'd laughed to himself.

But in the middle of it all Rose had got that

terrible disease and they'd had to cancel the cruise. She'd become very ill very quickly and soon could no longer manage their daily walks together so it had been just him and Gertie. Then Rose had died. He remembered going back to the house after the funeral. There'd been sandwiches and sausage rolls and drinks laid on at their local. Rose had wanted it to be a celebration of her life, with a proper party and lots of laughter. She'd said it cheered her to think of them all having fun, and had made all the arrangements herself with the help of Barbara, their daughter.

All their family and friends had been there to join in the celebration, though it was clear to Tom there was nothing to celebrate. He'd never felt so alone as he did among that throng of people, all telling him what a wonderful woman Rose had been. He didn't need them to tell him, and began to wish it would soon be over so he could go home and sit and just think about Rose.

Eventually the guests began to drift off, back to their own busy lives, and Barbara had offered to go back with him to keep him company for a while; she'd even offered to stay overnight if he wanted her to. He told her he'd rather be alone and not to worry and saw, briefly, the relief in her eyes. He'd walked into the empty house with a mixture of relief at being home, and dread at the silence awaiting him. Even Gertie was subdued and silent, as if she knew it was a time for stillness.

He'd slumped in his chair in front of the cold grate, having no heart to make a fire, and felt the emptiness surround him like a shroud. He had no illusions about meeting up with Rose again in the Afterlife; had never believed in all that guff, though Rose had taken comfort in the idea. Once it's over it's over, he'd told himself, and that's your lot.

After a while Gertie had put her head on his knee, whimpering softly. She'd looked up at him with her soft, trusting eyes, and he'd put his head in his hands and wept. She'd been a sort of comfort to him ever since, her simple needs giving him a reason to carry on.

And now some bastard had poisoned Gertie. Tom's sure it was one of the neighbours but he can't prove it and none of them will own up to it, the snivelling cowards. They were forever whining about her barking and messing on their precious lawns when she got out. So he cremated her on a bonfire at the bottom of the garden. Let them complain about the stink of burnt dog.

Tom arrives at the allotment and begins to tidy the beds, cutting back and digging up weeds where they've sprung up. Then he spends some time on his beloved roses; old varieties he's collected over the years which ramble over the hut.

You're not supposed to have any kind of building on the allotments but Tom's never cared about rules and regulations and he's had his allotment for years, long before these new people came in with their lists of rules. He'd built it himself from old off-cuts of wood and kept all his gardening tools there, together with a primus stove and provisions for making tea. You're not supposed to keep any tools there either, it encourages thieving, so they said, but he'd be damned if he was going to let them tell him what to do. In truth they never bothered him about it anyway. He reasoned that they probably thought that, at his age, he wouldn't be around much longer. Well, they weren't wrong there, he thinks bitterly.

After he's tidied, cutting away the dead wood and picking a few late blooms, Tom scatters the dog's ashes all around the roots. A fitting resting place, he thinks, wishing he could think of a few words to say, but instead he stands and looks around him, satisfied he's prepared the garden for its winter sleep.

Inside the hut he puts the kettle on the primus to make tea, arranges the blooms in an old jam jar he keeps on a bench under the window, and cuts slices of apple to nibble while waiting for the kettle to boil. The scent of roses engulfs him as he sips his tea, then he tosses the apple core outside onto the compost heap, and closes the door.

Arthur found him later that afternoon when he called round to share the latest gossip about the new allotment holders. They'd taken over Jim's plot after he'd died last year; a smart young couple with shiny wellies and shiny ideas to match. But they knew nothing about gardening. Tom and he had many a laugh at their expense and he was looking forward to passing on the latest news.

Arthur thought at first that Tom was asleep, his face looked so calm and peaceful. Then he noticed that he was half-sitting, half-lying with one arm inside the old bucket he used to fetch water from the stand-pipe. There was a deep gash down his forearm from which blood had flowed freely into the bucket. In Tom's other hand was a note on which Arthur could make out the three words: 'For the roses'.

Valentine

She took him for a three course Valentine
Special; two for the price of one with a
red rose thrown in, and a bottle of wine
which he quickly downed, then ordered another

on the firm understanding that she'd be
the driver. By the time they got to the
gateau he was smooth and mellow as he
leaned over the table and whispered a

thanks for the lovely meal and the wine and
all that, but isn't it time to be gone?
She finished hers quickly and, keys in hand,
led the way to her car for the drive home.

On reaching his flat she turned for a kiss,
he said thanks again, must rush, may've been
missed.

Failed Sonnet

I tried to write a sonnet about un-
requited love, where he proposed but she
refused his heartfelt plea, his bended knee
as merely tools of the patriarchy.

But despite best intentions on the part
of the writer, the bride insisted on
wearing white and tripping along, her heart
held out in hopeful anticipation

of their living happy-ever-after
in suburban wedded bliss. She said she
would obey! He promised to endow her
with all his worldly goods, including three

dozen shirts, all in need of ironing
by her fair hand, made his by a gold ring.

We welcome feedback and comments.

To contact Bare Writers:
barewriters@badice.co.uk

31240806R00099

Printed in Poland
by Amazon Fulfillment
Poland Sp. z o.o., Wrocław